This book is a work of fiction. Any references to historical events, real people, or real locales are used fictitiously.
Other names, characters, places, and incidents are the product of the author's imagination,
and any resemblance to actual events or locales or persons, living or dead, is entirely coincidental.
Based on the TV series Nickelodeon Avatar: The Last Airbender™ as seen on Nickelodeon ®

SIMON SPOTLIGHT
An imprint of Simon & Schuster Children's Publishing Division
1230 Avenue of the Americas, New York, New York 10020
The Earth Kingdom Chronicles: The Tale of Aang; The Earth Kingdom Chronicles: The Tale of Azula; The
Earth Kingdom Chronicles: The Tale of Toph; The Earth Kingdom Chronicles: The Tale of Sokka; © 2007
Viacom International Inc. All rights reserved. NICKELODEON, Nickelodeon Avatar: The Last Airbender,
and all related titles, logos, and characters are trademarks of Viacom International Inc.
All rights reserved, including the right of reproduction in whole or in part in any form.
SIMON SPOTLIGHT and colophon are registered trademarks of Simon & Schuster, Inc.
For information about special discounts for bulk purchases, please contact Simon & Schuster Special Sales at
1–866–506–1949 or business@simonandschuster.com.
Manufactured in the United States of America 0210 OFF
2 4 6 8 10 9 7 5 3 1
ISBN 978-1-4169-9446-6
The Tale of Aang Library of Congress Control Number 2006937729
The Tale of Azula Library of Congress Control Number 2006938027
The Tale of Toph Library of Congress Control Number 2007925258
The Tale of Sokka Library of Congress Control Number 2007922923
These titles were previously published individually by Simon Spotlight.

JOURNEYS

THROUGH THE EARTH KINGDOM

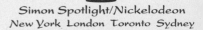

Simon Spotlight/Nickelodeon
New York London Toronto Sydney

INCLUDED IN THIS COLLECTION:

THE TALE OF AANG
THE TALE OF AZULA
THE TALE OF TOPH
THE TALE OF SOKKA

降世神通

AVATAR
THE LAST AIRBENDER.

THE EARTH KINGDOM CHRONICLES:
THE TALE OF
AANG

by Michael Teitelbaum
based on original screenplays
written for *Avatar: The Last Airbender*

Simon Spotlight/Nickelodeon
New York   London   Toronto   Sydney

Chapter 1

My name is Aang. I'm the Avatar. I'm also 5 an Airbender. My friend Katara has been teaching me Waterbending. She's become an amazing Waterbender!

Katara and her brother, Sokka, are traveling with me, helping me to master all four elements—air, water, earth, and fire—so I can defeat Fire Lord Ozai and the Fire Nation, and bring peace to the four nations. All in a day's work for the Avatar, right?

Next on my list is to learn Earthbending. So Katara, Sokka, my lemur Momo, and I are flying on my sky bison, Appa, to the city of Omashu in the Earth Kingdom to find my old pal King Bumi. I can't wait to learn Earthbending from him!

⊕ ⊕ ⊕

Our first stop was General Fong's Earth Kingdom base. He was supposed to give us an escort to make sure we made it to Omashu safely, but it didn't quite work out that way. General Fong had this crazy idea that he could force me into the Avatar state, and then I could go and fight the Fire Nation. He said that while I learn the elements, the war goes on. I started to think that maybe he was right, that maybe I could end the war now if I let him help me. Boy, was I wrong! Katara helped me realize how dangerous being in the Avatar state really is, especially when I can't control it. Even she's scared of me when I'm in it—that says a lot.

So I told General Fong that I wouldn't force the Avatar state. He flipped out! He told his Earth Kingdom soldiers to attack me so he could force me into it against my will. And when that didn't work, he attacked Katara. He started Earthbending her into the ground, so she was sinking. I was so angry and upset about Katara that the general got his wish: I went into the Avatar state, even though it took me a while to get into it. When I was in it, Avatar Roku, the previous Avatar, came to me. He told me that the Avatar state is a defense mechanism that gives me the skills and knowledge of all the past Avatars. In the Avatar state, all the spirits of past Avatars are within me. That is why I'm so powerful. But they are all exposed to whatever danger I face. If I'm killed while in the Avatar state, then all of the past Avatars will die with me. The reincarnation cycle will be broken and the Avatar will cease to exist. Pretty heavy, huh?

When I came out of the Avatar state, Katara was fine. I learned that Fong was just using her to trick me into going into the Avatar state. We finally managed to get away from him, thanks to Sokka, who snuck up behind him and conked him on the head with a club.

Anyway, after that was settled, we climbed onto the back of Appa, my flying bison. We're flying off toward Omashu—without an escort.

I'm trying not to think about what Roku told me—you know, about what would happen if I died in the Avatar state. Instead I'm turning my thoughts to Omashu and my old pal Bumi!

Chapter 2

8 After traveling for miles, Appa landed so we could rest for a bit. Katara was showing me a new Waterbending move called the Octopus. Things were going great until she put her arms around me to correct my form and I forgot everything I was doing and lost myself in her eyes. I can't help it—they're just so pretty! Anyway, that's when this singing and dancing group came walking out of the nearby woods. They told us they were nomads. We decided to travel with them to Omashu through these secret tunnels and caves that one of them, Chong, told us about. The tunnels cut through

the mountain and lead directly to Omashu.

As we entered the caves, Chong told us about the legend of the two lovers. He also told us that the caves were cursed.

"Only those who trust in love can make it through the caves. Everyone else gets trapped forever."

Hmm. All we have to do is trust in love? Something tells me that's harder than it sounds. . . .

As soon as we stepped into the cave, a rockslide sealed off the entrance. We wandered through the tunnels for hours. Then a wolfbat attacked. I sent an Airbending blast at it, which knocked Sokka's flaming torch from his hand and onto Appa, who started kicking wildly. I'd never seen him so upset! Katara put out the fire just as Appa kicked the cave walls and rocks came tumbling down from the ceiling. I managed to get Sokka and the nomads out of the way in time, but then the rest of the ceiling came crashing down, and I had to grab Katara and fly us to the other side of the cave. After the crash, I found myself on the ground next to Katara with my arm around her.

What are the odds? I wish I could stay like

this forever . . . but I have to get up and make sure everyone's okay. Looks like Appa's okay, and Katara is too, but what's that huge wall of rocks? Oh, no! The wall has separated us from Sokka and the nomads. I guess they're going to have to find their own way out of the tunnel—I have to focus on finding a safe way out for Appa, Katara, and me.

We'd been walking through the dark tunnels for hours when we came across a large stone door. We pushed through the door, but instead of an exit, there was a tomb—two tombs actually.

Katara noticed that the pictures on the tomb walls told the lovers' story. They were from warring villages on opposite sides of the mountain. Because of the war, the lovers had to meet in secret. They learned Earthbending from the badger moles so they could Earthbend these tunnels and caves to get to one another. Then the man was killed in the war. Instead of destroying both villages with her Earthbending power, the woman forced the two villages to stop the war and together they built a new city. The woman's name was Oma. The man's name was

Shu. And so the new city was named Omashu to honor their love.

"It says here 'Love is brightest in the dark,'" Katara read.

Her torch is starting to fade. Soon we'll be trapped in total darkness. For the first time since we entered the caves, I'm worried. Still, I don't want Katara to know how nervous I am. Just stay calm, and everything will be fine.

"I have a crazy idea," Katara said suddenly.

"What?" I hope it's a good one, because this place is giving me the creeps!

"Never mind," she said, turning away.

It's pretty dark in here, but is Katara blush—ing? It sure looks like it.

"It's too crazy."

"Katara, what is it?" One of us better come up with something soon. . . .

"Well, the curse says that we'll be trapped in here forever unless we trust in love. And above this picture of them kissing it says 'Love is brightest in the dark.' So, what if we kissed?"

Uh . . . did I just hear her right? Katara and me, kiss? Katara wants to kiss me? Almost since the moment I met her I've dreamed of kissing her. Did she really say that?

"Us, kissing?" I need to be sure I actually heard her right.

"See, that was a crazy idea," she said quickly.

This is going to be the best day of my life! I can't move, breathe, or smile, but I've never been more excited in my life! I think I may pass out. . . .

"Us. Kissing." Okay, stop saying that and just say yes before she changes her—

"Us, kissing!" Katara repeated, laughing loudly. "What was I thinking? Can you imagine that!"

It's too late. I blew it! Standing here in my daze I let the moment pass and now she's tak—ing the crazy wonderful suggestion back . . . like she wishes she never said it. Now I have to act that way too. I mean, I can't let her know that I think it's the greatest idea she ever had. Just smile, and try to sound like you agree with her.

"I definitely wouldn't want to kiss you!" Oh, no. I wish I could take that back. What a dumb thing to say! And I don't even mean it!

"Oh, well I didn't realize it was such a hor—rible option," Katara said harshly. "Sorry I suggested it."

Great, now she's mad. Why do I say such dumb things! I have to make this right.

"No, no, I mean if it's a choice between kissing you and dying, I—" Oh boy, that didn't help. I just can't get it right when it comes to Katara. Okay, let's try again.

"I'm saying I would rather kiss you than die. That's a compliment."

"Well, I'm not sure which I would rather do!"

And now she's storming out of the tomb. Great. Instead of fixing things, I just keep making them worse. Why am I so afraid to let Katara know how I feel about her? Now it doesn't matter. I really blew it.

"We're going to run out of light any second now, aren't we?" I asked, catching up to her.

"I think so."

At least she's still talking to me. "Then what are we going to do?"

"What can we do?" She turned toward me. Just then her light went out.

Here we are in pitch dark with no hope

of ever getting out, except to believe in the legend. To believe in love. I'm just going to go for it. Come on Aang, just be brave. What do you have to lose? Just lean in and . . .

Whoa! What's that path of light on the ceiling? I guess love really will show us the way! The lights look like some kind of crystal.

"They must only light up in the dark!" I realized.

"That's what they meant by love being brightest in the dark!" Katara exclaimed. "That's how the two lovers found each other. They put out their lights and followed the crystals."

So we followed the crystals all the way out of the caves. A moment after we exited, we saw Sokka and the nomads riding badger moles out of the cave. Then we said good-bye to the nomads and went on our way.

We are so close to Omashu, I can smell it! Just over this big hill and there it—no! I can't believe my eyes. There, draped over the main wall of the great Earth Kingdom city of Omashu, is a gigantic Fire Nation flag!

🏮 🏮 🏮

Things haven't exactly been going according to plan since we started this journey through the Earth Kingdom, and getting Bumi to teach me Earthbending was another one of those things. Even though Omashu was taken over by the Fire Nation, I insisted on going in anyway to find Bumi.

On our way through the city, we got attacked by a Firebender and ended up bumping into the Earth Kingdom resistance. I asked them about Bumi, and they said he surrendered the city on the first day of the invasion. That didn't sound like my old pal Bumi, so I didn't believe them at first; but now it makes more sense. See, while I looked for Bumi, Sokka and Katara evacuated the Earth Kingdom residents from the city by pretending they had all been infected with pentapox. Pentapi are harmless creatures that stick to you and make big purple marks on your skin—but the Fire Nation didn't know that! They thought the purple marks were contagious and let all the citizens leave. As they were leaving, Katara and Sokka noticed that the baby boy of the newly appointed Fire Nation governor of Omashu had followed them out of the city. We decided to have a trade—off: the baby for King Bumi. But just as we were about to make the trade, another

Firebender stepped forward and called it off. Then they pulled Bumi away. I chased after him, and in between dodging flying fireballs, I was able to have a brief talk with my old friend.

He told me that in addition to the positive and negative jings, or techniques, of attacking and retreating used in the bending arts, Earthbending also requires a neutral jing, which involves listening and waiting for the right moment to strike. He's using the neutral jing, just waiting for the right moment to attack. Then he'll take back Omashu when the Fire Nation least expects it. That sounds more like Bumi! He won't be teaching me Earthbending, but he did tell me I need to find someone who has mastered neutral jing. I need to find a teacher who waits and listens before striking.

I wonder when I'm going to see my old friend Bumi again . . . but in the meantime, I'm on a mission to find an Earthbending teacher who waits and listens before striking, just like Bumi said.

Chapter 3

We flew over the Earth Kingdom, not really sure where we were headed next. As we passed over a swamp, I heard it calling to me, telling me to land. I figured if I was actually hearing the Earth, I probably shouldn't ignore it.

A few seconds later, a fierce wind pulled us down toward the swamp. By the time we landed, we had all gotten separated. While I was on my own, I had this vision of a laughing girl in a white dress. She seemed to want me to follow her, and she just kept laughing as I chased her through the swamp. Then she disappeared.

The wind turned out to just be a Waterbender who was trying to protect the swamp. He told us that the swamp is actually just one giant tree that is connected to everything, that the entire world is connected, and that time is an illusion.

But if time really is an illusion, maybe the girl I saw was someone I will meet in the future. Sokka and Katara also had visions, only theirs were of people from their past. Hmm . . . sometimes I wish I were just plain smarter. It would sure come in handy as the Avatar!

🀄 🀄 🀄

Anyway, we left the swamp and went to the town of Gaoling to Master Yu's Earthbending Academy in search of a teacher. But all Master Yu did was try to sell me more lessons. That's when I realized he's definitely not the one!

Then I heard about an Earthbending tournament called Earth Rumble Six, where the top Earthbenders in town competed against one another. So we went to watch. It was like nothing I'd ever seen! Xin Fu, who was running it, kept introducing Earthbenders with names like the Boulder and the Gopher. Boy, were they huge! The Boulder had beaten everyone in sight so far! At first I thought the Boulder was the champion, but I really couldn't see him being the teacher Bumi was talking about. I'm pretty sure the Boulder doesn't ever wait or listen. Oh, here comes the Boulder's final opponent—she's a twelve-year-old blind girl! She calls herself the Blind Bandit. SHE'S actually the reigning champion. She must be incredible. I can't wait to watch her!

Just then the Blind Bandit began to laugh defiantly.

Wait a second—I've heard that laugh before! She's the girl from my vision in the swamp! The vision really was of someone from the future. I guess I'm pretty smart after all!

Then the most incredible thing yet happened—the Blind Bandit beat the Boulder! Every time the Boulder took a step, the Blind Bandit knew exactly where he was. She shifted her weight from one foot to the other. The small movement was powerful enough to create a ripple in the ground, which rushed toward the Boulder like a wave. As he put his foot down, the wave struck it, causing him to hit the ground with his legs split wide apart. Then the Blind Bandit forced three stone spikes to burst from the ground, slamming into the Boulder and knocking him from the ring. The match was over in a matter of seconds.

"Winner and still champion, the Blind Bandit!" Xin Fu shouted from the center of the arena.

"How did she do that?" Katara asked.

The answer struck me at once. "She waited, and she listened." Just like Bumi said.

Then the announcer offered gold to anyone from the audience who could beat her, and I volunteered. I just wanted to get close enough to ask her to be my Earthbending teacher, but she kept knocking me with Earthbending moves. Finally I had to knock her down with an Airbending blow. She was pretty angry and stormed out of the arena.

We finally tracked her down as a member of the Beifong family. She's royalty! Pretty strange, huh? Anyway, we traveled to the house of Lao and Poppy Beifong. What a mansion! It's on a huge estate with gardens, servants, and everything. I announced myself as the Avatar, and Katara, Sokka, and I were invited in for dinner. At the dinner table sat the Blind Bandit, whose real name is Toph Beifong. Master Yu, the head of the Earthbending Academy, was there too. He's Toph's Earthbending teacher—like she needs one!

Anyway, it turned out that her parents didn't have a clue how powerful an Earthbender she is. They still thought she was a beginner! After dinner she told me that even though her parents saw her blindness as a handicap and were more protective of her because of it, she's always been able to see by using her Earthbending. She feels vibrations through her feet and that tells her everything she needs to know—and way more than most of us can see.

In the end, she had to tell her parents the truth because we were ambushed by the Earthbenders from Earth Rumble Six—they wanted to steal back the gold I had won. It all worked out though, and Toph agreed to be my teacher! I'm so excited. I think she's going to be exactly the teacher that Bumi wanted me to have.

We're off on Appa, again, and for the first time in a while, things are finally starting to look up.

Chapter 4

One night in our camp, Toph rushed from her tent and woke us all. "There's something coming toward us."

Her supersensitive feet were picking up vibrations of something rumbling closer and closer.

"Should we leave?" Katara asked.

"Nature seems to think so," I said, watching tons of animals flee from the woods in terror. "Let's go."

We all climbed onto Appa and took off into the night sky. I caught a glimpse of what was chasing us. It was this strange machine made of metal and shaped like a tank, coughing up black smoke. I didn't know what it was, but I had a really bad feeling about it.

No matter how far or fast we went, it kept finding us! I finally guided Appa up a high mountain to a steep cliff.

It followed us to three different places before we finally decided to stand our ground and see who or what it was. Turns out it was these three Fire Nation girls who we had dealt with in Omashu, including the Firebender who had chased Bumi and me through the Omashu mail chutes. They began galloping toward us. Toph unleashed some spectacular Earthbending moves to block them, but they dodged the huge rocks and kept on coming. It was clear to me that we weren't going to stop them. So once again we climbed aboard Appa and took off.

I know how tired I am. I can only imagine how exhausted Appa must be, carrying all of us, flying all night with no sleep. Hmm . . . I wonder why it feels like we're flying downward? Appa! He's dozing off! Okay, now we have to land, no matter what. Appa needs to rest!

On the ground, Katara and Toph started arguing about whose fault all of this was.

"If this is anyone's fault, it's 'sheddy' over there," Toph yelled, pointing at Appa. "He's been shedding his fur and leaving a trail for those girls to follow!"

I can't believe my ears! That's so unfair! I don't care if she is my Earthbending teacher. Nobody talks about Appa like that when I'm around. "How dare you blame Appa! He saved your life three times today! You always talk about how you carry your own weight, but you don't. Appa does. He carries your weight. And you know what? He never had a problem flying when it was just the three of us!"

Oops. I think I went a bit too far. I didn't really mean it. I'm just exhausted, and I don't like anyone saying bad things about Appa. Still, I was a bit harsh. . . . I wonder what she'll say. . . .

"See ya," she said finally. Then she picked up her bag and disappeared into the forest.

"I can't believe I yelled at my Earthbending teacher and now she's gone. I just tossed away my best chance of beating the Fire lord, of saving the world . . . of doing my job as the Avatar."

"I was pretty mean to her too," Katara admitted. "We need to find her and apologize."

The worst part is, it turns out Toph is right! Appa is shedding like crazy. Now that I look I can see his fur everywhere. I need to come up with a plan. . . .

✦ ✦ ✦

First we washed Appa's shedding fur off in the river so that he wouldn't leave another trail. Then I told Katara and Sokka to take Appa and go find Toph. Meanwhile I grabbed a bunch of Appa's fur and flew around, leaving a fake trail in a totally different direction. This way if the tank follows the fur, it will be way off course. I hope I can make things right with Toph, but first I've got to stop those girls.

After flying around spreading Appa's fur, I landed in this town in the middle of nowhere. It's completely deserted. I should probably leave, but the thing is, I can't keep running forever, can I? I can't lose sight of my bigger mission. The time has come to face whoever is after me.

I think I'll just sit here and wait for them to find me, and find out what they're after. What's that sound? It's the Firebender! "All right, you've caught up with me. Now, who are you and what do you want?" It's time to settle this once and for all.

"Don't you see the family resemblance?" she asked. Then she covered one eye with her hand and said in a low gravelly voice, "I must find the Avatar to restore my honor."

Zuko! She sounds just like him. And now that I look closely, she looks kind of like him too. Is she Zuko's sister? Did they send her to track me down now? Did something bad happen to Zuko, and she took his place? Come to think of it, I haven't run into Zuko in a while. . . . Wait a minute, why am I worried about Zuko? He's devoted his life to trying to capture me for the Fire Nation. Besides, I'm the one in danger! I wonder if she's as powerful as he is.

"So, what now?" Let's see what she's made of.

"Now it's over," she said. "You can run, but I'll always catch you."

Like brother, like sister. "I'm not running."

"Do you really want to fight me?"

"Yes, I really do."

Okay, I know I didn't say that. Who—Zuko? Where did he come from? Has he been following me too? Are they going to team up against me?

"Back off, Azula," Zuko threatened. "He's mine."

Just back away slowly. The last thing I need is to face two Firebenders at the same time. Still, it doesn't seem like they're going to fight me as a team. They don't seem to like each other very much. It must be tough for Zuko to have a sister who seems so coldhearted. Wait a second—do I actually feel sorry for Zuko? Is that possible?

"I can see you two have a lot of catching up to do," I said. "So I'll just be going."

I guess I shouldn't have said anything. Just then, both Zuko and Azula turned toward me.

I can't escape. I'll have to battle them both. Zuko looks more anxious than me. Is he afraid of his sister? Azula is just smiling—her smile makes my skin crawl. There's no way out of this without fighting—I just hope I have the strength to make it out alive.

Azula just struck—but not me. I'm okay. She's attacking Zuko! Why are they so bent on attacking each other? Never mind, there's no time now. I have to protect myself.

Actually, I think the only thing keeping me alive this long is their desire to fight with each other—they keep forgetting I'm here! Wow. Azula just blasted Zuko through the wall of an abandoned building! I guess I actually do feel sorry for him. His sister is totally ruthless, and obviously a much more powerful Firebender than he is.

AHHH! I guess since Zuko's still recovering from Azula's blow, she can concentrate on me. I'm trapped in the corner of the blazing building. Stay calm, Aang. Just think—wait, where's that water coming from? It's splashing out the flames! "Katara!" Boy, am I glad to see her. Sokka's here too. Okay, Azula, watch out now. I've got backup.

Azula's holding her own against us. Gosh, she's really powerful.

Wait—why is the ground suddenly rumbling?

"I thought you guys could use a little help," Toph said, sending an Earthbending wave at Azula.

She's back! Boy, am I glad to see her! When this fight is over, I owe her a big apology. And a big thank-you. But first I have to survive this battle.

Just then Zuko's uncle Iroh showed up and helped Zuko to his feet. Then something kind of weird happened. It was like we all realized that Azula was trying to take on the whole world, and that even though we aren't all on the same side of this war, we needed to unite against her. So Katara, Sokka, Toph, Zuko, his uncle, and I formed a circle around Azula.

"I know when I'm beaten," she said. Finally she was surrendering!

But it turned out that she wasn't finished quite yet. She blasted her uncle with a bolt of lightning, and before we could get her back, she vanished. Katara offered to help heal Iroh with her powers, but Zuko refused her help. I can't believe he won't even work with us to help someone he loves. He probably feels humiliated and frustrated by having a sister who's trying to destroy him. But why can't we work together against her? It's strange—for a long time I feared Zuko, and now I kind of pity him.

Sokka, Katara, Toph, and I scrambled onto Appa, and off we flew. Before we settled down for some much-needed sleep, I apologized to Toph and thanked her for coming back.

"Let's see if you still thank me after tomorrow, twinkle toes," Toph said as she slipped into her earth tent. "That's when we begin your Earthbending lessons."

Chapter 5

"Good morning, Earthbending student," Toph said.

I leaped to my feet and snapped to attention. "Good morning, Sifu Toph."

"Hey!" Katara shouted, rubbing the sleep from her eyes. "You never call me Sifu Katara."

Oops! "Well, if you think I should . . . ," I replied, then I turned back to Toph.

"What are you going to teach me first?" I said, barely able to stand still. "Rock-a-lance? Making whirlpools out of land?"

"How about we start with 'move a rock'?" Toph suggested. "The key to Earthbending is your stance," she continued. "You must be steady and strong. Rock is a stubborn element. If you are going to move it, you've got to be firmly rooted—like a rock—yourself."

I watched Toph grip the ground with her toes, as if she were growing right into the earth. Then she swung her arms in a fluid motion and sent a huge boulder flying into the cliff wall. It exploded into a million pieces.

Man, she's good!

"Now you give it a try," Toph said.

I turned toward another boulder and set my feet. Steady, strong, stubborn, I thought. Then I swung my arms toward the boulder.

WHOOSH!

I went flying backward through the air, far away from the boulder I was trying to move. I landed fifty feet away from the thing, and it hadn't even budged!

It's just sitting there mocking me. What did I do wrong? I did exactly what Toph did, I think.

"Maybe if I came at the boulder from another angle, I could—"

"No!" Toph shouted. "That's the problem. Stop thinking like an Airbender. There is no different angle or clever solution or trick that's going to move that rock. You can't dance around the problem like you do with Airbending. You've got to face it head—on. Stay rooted. Be rocklike. I see we've got a lot of work to do."

Stop thinking like an Airbender? How can I do that? It's who I am. Instead of helping me, she's asking me to do the impossible. I didn't have this kind of trouble when Katara taught me Waterbending—I just picked it up immediately. But this is different. And so is Toph. She's not quite as understanding and sweet as Katara.

Next Toph made me run through an obstacle course with a heavy stone on my shoulder. I thought I was going to pass out. Then I had to shove my hands into a barrel of sand. Toph did it easily, but no matter how hard I tried, the sand kept scraping my skin and burning me.

Why is this so hard for me?

Then we tried combat, and I was even worse at that! Toph lunged at me, shouting, "Rock—like!" But I flinched backward, falling back on my old Airbending habits of retreat.

I'm not doing anything right! Maybe I should just quit before I get hurt.

"Stop thinking like an Airbender!" Toph shouted again and again.

I'm trying, but I've approached bending one way my whole life. I can't just force my instincts to change . . . can I?

After hours of practice, I finally made some progress. Toph had me toss a sack of rocks into the air, then move forward and catch it. And I did it! I kept doing it as I moved toward Toph, who was standing across the way. As I neared Toph, she lunged at me. But I stood my ground. I didn't flinch. I didn't jump back. I stayed rooted in my spot like a rock. Toph nodded at me in approval.

I think I might float away, I'm so happy. Of course, that wouldn't be rocklike.

I didn't stay happy for too long. We were at the bottom of a long ramp that Toph had created, and I could see a huge boulder resting at the top of it.

"I'm going to roll that boulder down at you," Toph explained. "If you have the attitude of an Earthbender, you'll stay in your stance and stop the rock."

I suddenly feel sick to my stomach. What happens if I can't do it? Stopping a rolling boulder seems much tougher than simply moving one.

"Sorry, Toph," Katara said, "but are you sure this is really the best way to teach Aang Earthbending?"

"Actually, Katara, there is a better way," Toph said.

Phew! Thank you, Katara! Maybe I won't have to stop that boulder after all. Wait a minute—why is Toph tying a blindfold around my eyes? She can't be serious?

"This way you'll have to sense the vibration of the boulder to stop it," Toph said.

Oh, great! Big help, Katara! Now I'll really get flattened. Okay, just take a deep breath, root your feet to the ground, and set your stance, hands extended in front of you. You are going to stop that boulder, Aang, even with this blindfold on.

Then Toph gave it an Earthbending shove.

Hey, I CAN feel the vibrations through my feet. It's rolling down. I CAN feel the boulder picking up speed. It's close, getting closer, just a few inches away. AHHH! I have to get out of the way! This rock is going to crush me! I just know it. I can't move it! I can't stop it. I'm just not an Earthbender—that's all there is to it! Jump! Jump! Save yourself!

Then the boulder rolled harmlessly past.

"You blew it!" Toph yelled. "You had a perfect stance and perfect form, but when it came
right down to it, you just didn't have the guts!"

She's right. I blew it. What kind of Avatar
am I?

"I know. I'm sorry."

"You ARE sorry. You're a jelly-boned wimp.
Now, do you have what it takes to face that
rock like an Earthbender?"

Why does she have to yell at me all the
time? Why does she have to make everything
so hard? She treats me like I'm a little kid, and
like she's the greatest thing that ever lived. I
can't stand it anymore.

"No," I replied, turning away. "I don't think I
have what it takes."

Katara suggested that we work on some Waterbending. I honestly don't feel like doing much of
anything. But Katara's being so nice to me, and
working on some Waterbending might lift my
spirits. Anything to get away from my failure for
a little while. Anything to forget how much I stink
at Earthbending, and how mean Toph is.

"You know this block you're having is only

temporary, right?" Katara said.

I knew she couldn't go long without bringing it up.

"I don't want to talk about it."

"That's the problem, Aang. If you face this issue instead of avoiding it, that's the Earthbender way."

"I know! I get it, all right? I need to face it head-on, like a rock. Be rocklike. I know. But I just can't do it. I don't know why I can't, but I can't."

I wish everyone would just leave me alone! But of course, she won't.

"Aang, if fire and water are opposites, then what's the opposite of air?"

"I guess it's earth."

"That's why it's so hard for you to get this. You're working with your natural opposite. But you'll figure it out. I know you will."

I never actually thought about it that way. But it seems to make sense. Maybe the key to getting Earthbending is to think and do the opposite of what I've always done as an Airbender. Could it be as simple as that? I think I can do that. At least I can try again.

Just when I started feeling better, Toph started acting up. First she took some nuts from my bag without asking. I really didn't mind that—I'm always happy to share. But then she started using my antique staff, which was handcrafted by the monks, as a nutcracker. That kind of bothered me.

I think she's intentionally trying to make me mad. She probably thinks it will trigger some deep well of Earthbending power or something. Thing is, I'm not really mad. Sharing is just part of who I am. But I might ask her to leave my staff alone. Maybe later—I'm not ready for another confrontation with her right now.

Just then Katara came to tell me that she couldn't find Sokka. We split up to search and I found him stuck in a hole in the ground. I tried to Airbend him out, but all I ended up doing was blowing dust in his face.

"Aang, I know you're new at it," Sokka said, "but I could use a little Earthbending here!"

I just can't. What if I try and fail again? I'd feel like an even bigger loser. I suppose I could go get Toph, but that would be like admitting I'm a great big failure.

Just then an angry saber-toothed moose

lioness came looking for her cub, which Sokka had been playing with before he fell in the hole.

"Aang, this is bad!" Sokka said, panicking. "You've got to get me out of here!"

Okay, this is serious. Sokka's life is at stake. I have to stop feeling sorry for myself and just do what Toph's been telling me. It's time to start thinking like an Earthbender and get Sokka out of there!

My feet are planted. I am not about to move, no matter what, not even now that the beast is charging right at me. Wait—she's stopping! She's turning around and walking away. Did I make her leave? Was my will so rocklike that she couldn't stand up to me?

Then Toph jumped out from behind the bushes.

She's been watching the whole time? "Why didn't you help us?" I asked. I can't believe she put us both in such danger.

"Guess it just didn't occur to me," she said as she dropped a nut onto the ground and went to smash it with my staff.

That does it. Now I AM mad. That staff is important to me and she has no right to treat it that way. "Enough!" I reached out and grabbed the staff before it struck the ground. "I want my staff back. Now!"

"Do it!" Toph shouted, letting go of the staff. "Do it now!"

"Do what?"

"Earthbend, twinkle toes! You just stood your ground against a crazed beast, and even more impressive, you stood your ground against me. You've got the stuff! Now do it!"

As bossy as she was being, I knew she was probably right. So I set my feet and focused my mind. Then I whipped my arms around in an Earthbending move and sent a bunch of big rocks flying.

"You did it!" Toph cried. "You're an Earthbender!"

She's proud of me! Actually, I'm kind of proud of myself. I can't believe I did it. I AM an Earthbender. I turned to set Sokka free with an Earthbending move, but Toph stopped me.

"You should probably let me do that. You're still a little new to this and you might accidentally crush him."

Chapter 6

Today we met this professor of anthropology who was looking for this legendary library. It's supposed to have more books than any other in the world. Sokka thought that it might have a map of the Fire Nation, or just some information that would be helpful. So we decided to go with him to find the library. When we found the library, Sokka, Katara, the professor, Momo, and I went inside while Toph waited outside with Appa.

Inside, Sokka made an amazing discovery— Firebenders lose their power during a solar eclipse because the sun is covered up! Then we were able to calculate the date of the next solar eclipse using this incredible calendar.

"If we attack the Fire Nation on that date, they'll be helpless," cried Sokka. "We've got to get this info to the Earth King at Ba Sing Se!"

Unfortunately the spirit of the library over-heard Sokka, and he was so angry that we were using his knowledge for our own purposes that he decided to sink the library into the desert to keep its knowledge from humans.

The professor decided to stay, surrounded by all the world's knowledge, but thankfully Sokka, Katara, and I got out just as the library disappeared into the sand.

⊕ ⊕ ⊕

We're finally outside. Phew! But the strange thing is, I can't see Appa anywhere. There's Toph. . . . Where could he have gone? And why does Toph look so serious?

"Where's Appa?" She's not responding. . . . That's a bad sign.

"Toph, what happened?" Oh, no! I have this horrible sinking feeling rising from the pit of my stomach. "Where's Appa?"

I listened in horror as Toph told me that when

the library started sinking, she used all her Earth-bending abilities to hold it up until we got out. While she was doing that, a group of Sandbenders kidnapped Appa and took him away.

I feel like a piece of my own body has just been ripped out. I can't remember a time in my life when Appa wasn't by my side. And now he's gone! Gone!

"How could you let them take Appa!" I don't care if she's my Earthbending teacher. I just want Appa back! "Why didn't you stop them?"

"I couldn't," she replied weakly. "The library was sinking, and you guys were still inside. I would have lost all of you if I stopped to save Appa. I can hardly feel any vibrations out here in the sand. The Sandbenders snuck up on me and I didn't have time to—"

"You just didn't care! You never liked Appa! You wanted him gone!"

Enough excuses! I can't believe this—what if I never get him back?

Then Katara stepped between us. "Aang, stop it! You know Toph did all she could. She saved our lives!"

Now Katara's turned against me! This is just

too much. "That's all any of you guys care about—yourselves! You don't care if Appa is okay!"

I've never felt more alone. My lifelong buddy is gone. My friends have all turned on me. It's obvious I'm not going to get any help. I'm going to have to find Appa myself.

"I'm going after Appa." I whipped open my glider. Then I turned to Toph. "Which direction did they go?"

Toph shrugged and pointed. I looked at the ground and saw a trail left by the sand sailer the Sandbenders must have been riding.

"I'll be back when I find him." Then I leaped into the sky.

I'm so upset, I could cry. I don't know what I'll do if he's really gone. How can your best friend in the whole world be there one second and then just be gone the next? It doesn't make any sense. Come on, Aang. Keep looking. Find him!

I followed the tracks for a little while, but soon they were wiped away by the desert winds. I flew over the desert for hours, searching in every direction, but it was no use.

I glided to a landing back where the library was, and Katara came over and placed her hand on my shoulder. "I'm sorry, Aang. I know it's hard for you right now, but we need to focus on getting out of here."

I don't feel like focusing on anything but Appa. Nothing matters at all. Not my friends, not being the Avatar, not saving the world. Not even getting out of this desert alive. "What's the difference? We won't survive without Appa. We all know it."

Katara kept trying to cheer me up, but I was barely listening. People call me the last Airbender, but that's not really true. Appa was—is—an Airbender too. Nobody, not even Katara, understands him the way I do. To everyone else he's just a big furry animal. But I know that he's a special being, as close to me as any of my human friends.

Suddenly Katara grabbed my hand and pulled me up to my feet.

"Aang, get up. We're getting out of this desert."

She seems really adamant about leaving. I really don't care either way. Without Appa, nothing matters.

Katara decided that it would be better if we rested during the day and traveled at night, using the stars to navigate our way to Ba Sing Se. As we walked, Toph stubbed her toes on something in the sand. It turned out to be a sand sailer.

"It's got a compass on it," Katara said excitedly. "Aang, if you can bend a breeze, we can sail to Ba Sing Se. We're going to make it!"

I felt a little better that we weren't all going to die out there. But not much. I used my Airbending to power the sail and we glided across the desert until all of a sudden, we were attacked by buzzard-wasps. Then, out of nowhere, a huge sandstorm rose up, blowing the creatures away. When the storm died down, we saw that a group of Sandbenders had whipped up the storm to save us.

But I'm in no mood to say thanks. It was Sandbenders who took Appa. . . .

"What are you doing in our land with what looks like a stolen sand sailer?" the leader of the Sandbenders demanded.

"We're traveling with the Avatar. Our bison was stolen and we have to get to Ba Sing Se," Katara replied. "We found the sailer abandoned in the desert."

"You dare accuse our people of theft when you ride in a stolen sand sailer?" yelled a younger Sandbender angrily.

"Quiet, Ghashiun!" an older man shouted. "No one accused our people of anything!"

"Sorry, Father," Ghashiun said, stepping back.

Toph leaned in close to me. "I recognize the son's voice, and I never forget a voice," she whispered. "He's the one who stole Appa."

I rushed toward Ghashiun, my anger rising quickly. "You stole Appa!" I shouted, boiling with rage. "Where is he? What did you do to him?"

"They're lying!" Ghashiun cried. "They're the thieves!"

These people are going to tell me where Appa is or pay a heavy price! I'll show them how serious I am with a massive Airbending blast to one of their sand sailers—

BAM!

It shattered into splinters. The Sandbenders backed away, stunned.

"Where is my bison?"

"It wasn't me!" Ghashiun cried.

"You said to put a muzzle on him!" Toph shouted.

"You muzzled Appa?!" I can barely control myself. The thought of it makes me want to scream!

I fired an Airbending blast at another sand sailer, then turned my sights on the Sandbenders themselves. Usually the thought of fighting another person is against everything I believe in, against everything the monks taught me. I'm sorry, but I can't control myself from using force against these people. . . .

"I'm sorry!" Ghashiun cried. "I didn't know it belonged to the Avatar!"

"Tell me where Appa is!"

"I traded him to some nomads. He's probably in Ba Sing Se by now. They were going to sell him there."

Appa for sale, like some piece of meat? I can't take it anymore. I'm so angry, I could . . . I could . . .

My anger overcame me and I slipped into the Avatar state. After a while, I felt a strange calm wash over me as I left my body and rose above the desert floor. Looking down, I could see that my wrath had stirred up vicious desert winds whipping everyone below. I saw Sokka grab Toph and pull her away from me. I saw the Sandbenders running from me in terror. Then I saw my body standing in the center of the whirlwind.

But Katara, fighting the wind with each step, slowly made her way toward me. She didn't seem afraid of me this time. She just took hold of my body and hugged me. She didn't say a word.

Gradually my anger subsided and I saw the winds die down. Then I felt myself returning to earth, to my body. Katara did something for me that words could not do. The simple act of hugging me told me that she was there for me completely, without judgment, without lectures, without fear. It struck a chord deep inside me. I felt my heart open up to her. . . .

Then the wind stopped. But the pain I'd been keeping at bay rushed in with the force of a hurricane. I closed my eyes, gave myself over to Katara's arms, and cried harder than I had ever cried in my life.

Chapter 7

I did my best to push Appa out of my mind. I tried to focus all my thoughts and energy on getting to Ba Sing Se to tell the Earth King about the solar eclipse.

We finally got out of the desert and arrived at a waterfall pond. We ended up traveling across this stretch of land called Serpent's Pass, along with a refugee family that we met on the way. Serpent's Pass was definitely scary, but we made it through safely.

Katara keeps asking me about Appa, and I want to talk about it, but after what happened back in the desert, I'm trying to stay as unemotional as possible. The Avatar state is really dangerous, and until I know how to control it, I'd rather not get angry or upset enough to go into it again. I guess it's hard for Katara to understand that, though. She's all about feelings, and stuff like that.

Did I mention that one of the members of the refugee family is pregnant? Well, she just went into labor. It's pretty lucky we're off Serpent's Pass, huh? Katara has taken charge and is delivering the baby now; she used to help Gran Gran deliver babies back home. Wait, I just heard crying . . . it's a boy!

Now I'm inside the tent. There are the mom and dad, cuddling their newborn son. The baby is the most beautiful thing I've ever seen! It's amazing to watch them celebrate in the midst of all this pain and fighting, but I think the new life came to remind us that life goes on no matter what. I guess this is what living is all about: loving and caring for your family.

Sometimes I forget that I have a family now too—Katara, Sokka, Momo, and Appa. Even Toph. Just because Appa is missing, that doesn't mean I should stop caring about everyone else I love in my life. In fact, losing Appa has actually made me realize that I should show them how much I care about them, because we never know what might happen. It's okay for me to miss Appa. It's okay for me to feel sad, and to lean on Katara for help. That's what family is for, right?

"I've been going through a really hard time lately," I told the family. "But you've made me hopeful again."

Katara took my hand and smiled sweetly. My heart is beating so fast I can hardly breathe! "I thought I was trying to be strong, Katara. But I was really just running away from my feelings. Seeing this family together, so full of happiness and love, reminded me of how I feel about Appa."

Come on Aang, you can do it. . . .

"And how I feel about you." That's what I should have said in the Cave of Two Lovers. . . . Oh well, I hope I've at least redeemed myself from that!

Katara burst into tears. I guess I really do have a family. A pretty good one, too, if you ask me!

I said good-bye, then Momo and I took off to find Appa. "I promise, I'll find Appa as fast as I can. I just really need to do this. I'll see you all in Ba Sing Se."

Chapter 8

52 We're almost at the outer wall of Ba Sing Se. I can't wait to find Appa! Wait, what's that? Oh, no! A huge Fire Nation invasion force is marching toward the city! There must be thousands of tanks and troops advancing toward the outer wall. And what's that? Some kind of huge metal drill? This can only mean one thing: They're planning on drilling right through the outer wall of Ba Sing Se to invade the city. This is awful! I have to warn the others!

"Sorry, Momo. Appa's going to have to wait."

I met my friends right outside Ba Sing Se's outer wall and told them about the drill. Toph and

I Earthbended a ledge of rock up the side of the outer wall so that everyone could climb up and see the scary-looking drill moving closer and closer.

Once inside the gates, I marched up to the first guard I could find. I told him that I was the Avatar and he should take me to whoever was in charge. Then the three Firebenders who were following us showed up and attacked the Earth Kingdom soldiers. One of them, Ty Lee, actually takes people's chi away, leaving them unable to bend. Pretty scary stuff.

Anyway, Sokka has a plan to stop the drill by hitting its pressure points. The drill is made up of an inner section and an outer one. We figure if we cut through the braces, the whole thing will collapse.

As we walked back toward the drill, Toph whipped up a dust storm so that we wouldn't be seen. When the drill was directly above us, Sokka, Katara, Momo, and I jumped onto it. Toph stayed outside to slow the drill down from there with her Earthbending.

We're making our way through the drill; it's a twisting maze of pipes and valves. It's turning out to be too hard to cut through them completely, so we're just going to weaken them, and then I'll go up to the top of the drill and deliver a final Air-bending blow. Then the whole thing will collapse!

It sounds simple enough, but the thing is, everyone inside the city is depending on this plan succeeding. Once again, it's all up to me, the Avatar. I just hope that I won't let them down. . . .

🝗 🝗 🝗

One by one we hurried from brace to brace, slashing each one with our waterwhips until it was weakened. Just as we were finishing with the final brace, the three firebenders—Azula, Mai, and Ty Lee—launched an attack on us.

"Split up!" I cried. Katara tossed me her water pouch, then she and Sokka dashed down a corridor. Ty Lee and Mai followed them. Azula stayed behind.

"The Avatar's mine!" she cried.

I don't have time for this now—I have to complete our plan! Momo and I are dashing through the tank—we're finally at the top. Oh, no! The drill is already boring into the outer wall—the last line of the Earth Kingdom's defense!

I used Katara's water to slash an X-shaped

54

cut into the top of the drill's armor in preparation for my final blow. That's when Azula caught up with me and unleashed blast after blast of fire. I deflected what I could by Airbending, but when I tried to stop her with a water whip, she evaporated my supply! No matter what I did, she had me backing up.

Is Azula just too powerful for me to defeat? I actually feel sorry for Zuko now, having to deal with such a ruthless enemy, not to mention sister! Zuko is dangerous, but at least he has a decent reason for always trying to capture me: to get back into the good graces of his father, the Fire Lord. Azula is just plain crazy. It's like she enjoys hurting people and destroying things—as if she finds that fun, not just a necessary part of war. That ruthlessness makes her a much more dangerous opponent than Zuko ever could be. I'd take Zuko over his cold-blooded sister any day.

Azula keeps firing at me. I just need to keep fighting. . . . Azula may be more powerful than me, but I have to be smarter. I HAVE to stop her so I can bring down the drill.

Yes! She stumbled. Now's my chance . . .

While Azula struggled to regain her balance,

I grabbed a big rock. I Earthbended the rock in half, sharpening one end into a point. Then I rested the point in the X-shaped cut. I just needed some momentum for this to work. . . .

Just as Azula got back to her feet, I dashed down the wall, leaped into the air, and came down with all my might. Using a powerful Earthbending blow, I slammed my hands into the top of the rock spike I had made and left on top of the X-shaped cut in the drill.

BOOM!

The spike dug into the hull with such force that the weakened braces split and the whole machine broke apart. A river of slurry shot from the hole I had created, knocking Azula off the machine. I hopped onto the slurry and rode the wave down, like a surfer.

Woohoo! This is so great! The drill has been destroyed, the Fire Nation attack has been stopped, and the city is safe.

I almost feel free again, like I used to feel all the time when I went penguin sledding, and riding giant porpoises just for fun—before this war started, before Azula. I kind of feel like I'm just Aang again, not Aang the Avatar.

Chapter 9

In order to travel from the outer wall into the city, we rode a train along a monorail. When we got off at the Ba Sing Se train station, we stepped out onto a busy platform. My thoughts drifted back to Appa. I'd been so caught up in getting to Ba Sing Se, then in stopping the Fire Nation attack and destroying the drill, that I didn't allow myself time to think about my buddy. But we're here now, where he's been taken, and I promise I'm NOT going to leave this city without him.

At the station a woman came up to us and introduced herself as Joo Dee. She already knew who we were. She said it was her job to show us around the city, and so off we went in a fancy carriage pulled by a team of ostrich horses. As we rode, Sokka tried to explain to Joo Dee that we had important information for the king about the Fire Nation. But each time he brought it up, she changed the subject or ignored him.

"You're in Ba Sing Se now," she said. "Everyone is safe here."

Actually, before I got here Ba Sing Se was about to be invaded by the Fire Nation and their giant drill, but she just won't listen. Ba Sing Se is turning out to be a really strange city. There are three different sections: the lower, middle, and upper rings. They are divided by classes; the poorest people live in the lower ring and the richest live in the upper. I don't think I'm comfortable with that. I mean, I grew up listening to the monks teaching about equality and sharing.

Anyway, Joo Dee brought us to the upper ring. She pointed out the king's royal palace, and the Dai Li agents around it. Apparently the Dai Li is the cultural authority of the city. Then she showed us our new house. I wasn't planning on staying here long, but she said we have to wait a month before our appointment with the king!

We decided we'd spend the time looking for Appa. We had hoped that Joo Dee would leave us alone, but she insisted on escorting us all over. It didn't matter anyway; we didn't get very far.

I had such a strong feeling that Appa was there, but nobody we asked seemed to be able to help us find him!

After a totally frustrating day, Joo Dee finally dropped us off at our house. We met our next-door neighbor, Pong, hoping maybe we could get some answers from him. He was friendly enough, but as soon as we mentioned the war, he began trembling and looking around to see if he was being watched.

"Listen," he said, obviously frightened. "You can't mention the war in Ba Sing Se. And whatever you do, stay away from the Dai Li." Then he ran into his house and slammed the door behind him.

No one in this city will talk about anything important. It seems like some kind of conspiracy or something.

"We have to see the Earth King," Sokka insisted. "That's the only way to straighten this out."

Sokka's right. The king HAS to help us. I'm sure of it. And I'm NOT waiting a whole month in this weird city to see him!

A little while later, Katara was reading the paper and discovered that the king was having a party. She suggested that we sneak in and try to talk to him there. So she and Toph get to dress up like fancy society ladies, while Sokka and I have to pretend that we're busboys. The things I have to do sometimes!

We snuck in and spotted the Earth King, but on our way to him we were caught by Dai Li agents and taken to a library inside the palace. Then this guy approached me. He said his name was Long Feng, and that he was the grand secretariat of Ba Sing Se, cultural minister to the king, and head of the Dai Li. I asked him why he wouldn't let us see the king, and told him about the Fire Nation drill and the solar eclipse, but he didn't seem to care! He just said that the king had no time to get involved with politics or military activities, which makes no sense! What else does the king DO? All that stuff is his job. ESPECIALLY during a war. He said that silencing talk of the conflict made Ba Sing Se a peaceful, orderly utopia. Talk about crazy—this guy's nuttier than General Fong for sure!

Unfortunately, yelling at Long Feng just made him angrier at me. He told me he knew I was looking for Appa, and made it seem like he had the power to help, or to make it impossible. . . . Does he know where Appa is? I think Long Feng knows a lot more than he lets on. I need to find out what this guy is hiding, but it's going to take a little bit of planning. Right now, I just have to be calm.

And now there's this strange woman who wants to escort us home.

"What happened to Joo Dee?" Katara asked.

"I'm Joo Dee," the woman said, smiling. "I'll be your host as long as you're in our wonderful city!"

Just when I thought things couldn't get any stranger. What in the world is going on in this crazy city?

Chapter 10

My mind is racing and I can't slow it down. I'm trying really hard to figure out the next step to take so that we can find Appa. I'm trying to understand why nobody in this city wants to talk about a war that's on the verge of destroying their home—and the rest of the world! What is with these people?

Katara, Sokka, Toph, and I decided to go put up MISSING BISON posters all around the city, in the hopes that maybe someone had seen Appa somewhere. When we got back home, someone knocked on the front door. I was certain it would be someone with good news about Appa. But to my disappointment, it was only Joo Dee—the first Joo Dee—holding one of our posters. When we asked her where she had been, she told us that she took a short vacation at a place called Lake Laogai. Weird! Then she told us that we were forbidden to put up posters.

What CAN you do in this city? Anyway, I'm done listening to these people. It's obvious they don't want to help us, so we'll just help ourselves.

"We don't care about the rules, and we're not asking permission. We're finding Appa on our own, and you should just stay out of our way!" I slammed the door in her face. "From now on we do whatever it takes to find Appa."

We headed out of the house, more determined than ever. Then—I couldn't believe it—Katara ran into Jet, this rebel we had met earlier in our travels. What's he doing in Ba Sing Se? Now that I think back on it, Katara kind of had a crush on Jet—until he put a whole innocent village in danger trying to fight the Fire Nation! That's when Katara decided that she wanted nothing to do with him. I don't mind that part at all.

"I'm here to help you find Appa," said Jet.

He told Katara that he had changed, that he had given up his gang. I know she doesn't trust him, but at this point I really need all the help that I can get.

Jet led us to a warehouse where he had heard Appa had been taken. But when we got there, it was empty. At first Katara thought it was a trap, but then we found some of Appa's fur on the ground.

"They took that big thing yesterday," said a voice from a dark corner of the building. A janitor pushing a broom stepped into the light. "Some rich guy on Whaletail Island bought him—maybe for a zoo, or maybe for the meat."

FOR THE MEAT! I have to sit down. This feeling in my stomach is not good. . . . The idea of someone buying Appa for meat made me nauseous and furious at the same time. Appa is the last of a noble, proud breed, not somebody's dinner. I wasn't going to let anything happen to him! "We've got to get to Whaletail Island right away!"

Sokka looked it up on his map and discovered that it was really far away, back near the

South Pole. But I don't care how far away it is or how long it takes to get there. If there's a chance to find Appa, we have to take it.

On our way out of the warehouse, we ran into the members of Jet's gang, who told us that Jet had been arrested and dragged away by the Dai Li a few weeks earlier. Jet denied it and looked at them like they were crazy. He also denied being part of the gang altogether. Toph is kind of like a human lie detector, and she studied their heartbeats and breathing patterns and told us that both Jet and his gang friends were telling the truth.

"They both THINK they're telling the truth," Sokka realized suddenly. "That's because Jet's been brainwashed by the Dai Li!"

We grabbed Jet and brought him back to his apartment, where we tried to jog his memory.

"The Dai Li must have sent Jet and that janitor to mislead us," Katara said.

That made perfect sense! They wanted us out of Ba Sing Se, because we were stirring up trouble with our talk about the war, so they brainwashed Jet to lead us far away.

"I bet they still have Appa right here in the city!" I said, feeling hopeful again. "Maybe he's in the same place they took Jet!" I leaned in close to Jet. "Where did they take you?"

"Nowhere!" he cried, squirming in his chair. "I don't know what you're talking about!"

Katara used the water from her pouch and formed a sparkling band of healing energy around Jet's head to jog his memory. Slowly he began to relax.

"They took me to Dai Li headquarters," he said finally. "It was underwater, under a lake."

"Joo Dee said she went on a vacation to Lake Laogai," Sokka recalled.

"That's it!" Jet cried. "Lake Laogai!"

I'm certain now that's where we'll find Appa. I hope that we won't be too late. I don't know what I'll do if—NO, Aang, don't think that way! We WILL find Appa, and he'll be all right.

🀄 🀄 🀄

Sokka, Katara, Toph, Momo, and I traveled to Lake Laogai, along with Jet and two members of his gang, Longshot and Smellerbee. It was a big, beautiful lake surrounded by a thick woods. But there was no sign of a head—

66

quarters or any kind of passageway leading under the water.

Then Toph found a rock hatch in the water at the edge of the shore. She Earthbended the hatch open and revealed a stairway leading down under the lake. We hurried down the stairs and into a tunnel.

"It's coming back to me now," Jet said. "I think there's a cell big enough to hold Appa just ahead."

We're so close now. He might even be right around the next bend!

We made our way along the tunnel, which had rooms and holding cells on either side. In one of the rooms I saw a bunch of women all being trained—brainwashed, actually—to be Joo Dees. It was so creepy, like they were all preprogrammed robots. Yuck!

Continuing along the tunnel, we soon came to a door where Jet stopped. "I think it's through here," he said, flinging open the door.

Wait a second—this isn't Appa's cell. It's a room filled with Dai Li agents. There's Long Feng! Did Jet lead us into a trap, or did he just make an honest mistake?

"By breaking into our headquarters you have made yourselves enemies of the state," Long Feng announced. Then he turned to his agents. "Take them into custody!"

The Dai Li agents attacked, but we fought back. Then Long Feng started running, and Jet and I took off after him. We followed him back down the tunnel and into another room, where he slammed the door and turned to confront us. Jet is definitely on our side.

"All right, Avatar," Long Feng snarled confidently. "This is your last chance—if you want your bison back."

He does have Appa! I knew it! I could strike him down right where he stands, but not before I learn where he's holding my buddy.

"Tell me where Appa is!"

"Agree to exit the city now, and I'll waive all charges and allow you to leave with your lost pet," Long Feng said.

"You're in no position to bargain!" Jet shouted, drawing his twin hook swords.

"Definitely not," I added, taking up a combat stance beside Jet. If Long Feng wants to do this the hard way, I'll gladly accommodate him.

Then he looked Jet right in the eye and said, "Jet, the Earth King has invited you to Lake Laogai."

Jet's expression is completely changing— his eyes are narrower, and he's staring blankly ahead. What's happening to him?

"I am honored to accept his invitation," Jet said in a flat emotionless voice.

Long Feng just said the phrase that triggers Jet's brainwashing! This is not good!

A second later Jet attacked me, and Long Feng ran toward the door. I tried to stop Jet without hurting him, while doing my best to avoid the pointy tips of his swords.

"Jet, it's me, Aang. I'm your friend! You don't need to do this!"

Uh-oh, I'm not getting through to him! He just keeps lunging at me with his swords, and I can't keep dodging them forever. . . .

"Jet, look inside your heart. He can't make you do this—you're a freedom fighter!"

Wait! I think I may have just jogged his memory. He's stopped attacking me and he's just standing there staring . . . and now he's attacking Long Feng! Finally we're making progress!

I was about to help Jet fight Long Feng, but everything happened so fast, and before I knew it, Long Feng had blasted Jet with an Earthbending move that took him to the ground. Then Long Feng Earthbended himself out of the cave, and the whole gang rushed into the cave to find Jet hurt and lying on the ground. Katara tried to heal him, but Smellerbee and Longshot told us to go find Appa. They vowed to take care of him. Katara looked so upset, and even though Jet promised her he'd be all right, I wonder if he will be. We had to get to Appa before Long Feng did, so we left them and rushed down the tunnel until we came to a big holding cell. But we were too late. It was empty. Broken chains dangled from the wall. Appa's fur was everywhere.

"He's gone! Long Feng beat us here!" Again, I was too late. He'd been right here and I'd missed him.

"Maybe we can catch them," Sokka said, urging us on.

We raced back up the stairs and out of the headquarters. Back on the lake's shore we were surrounded by Dai Li troops.

It's over. We failed. I'm sorry, buddy. I let you down.

Just then, Momo started screeching like crazy and took off into the sky. When I looked up to see where he was going, I saw the most beautiful sight I'd ever seen. There, swooping majestically through the sky, is Appa.

He's alive! He's safe! He's free! He hasn't become somebody's pet or slave or dinner. Here's my buddy, back again at last. I'm so happy, I could cry!

"Appa!" I yelled.

Appa's reply came in the form of a huge Airbending blast that flattened the Dai Li troops. It turned out that when Long Feng had tried to take on Appa, Appa bit him on the leg and tossed him into the lake.

That's my buddy!

I leaped into the sky and landed on Appa's neck, hugging him with all my might. When my friends were all aboard, I shouted, "Yip, yip!" for the first time in weeks, and we took off into the sky.

"I missed you, buddy, more than you'll ever know."

Chapter 11

We finally made it inside the palace and into the throne room of the Earth King.

"We need to talk to you!" I said to the king. Then I spotted Long Feng standing at the king's side.

Great. I thought we got rid of this guy.

"He's lying!" Long Feng shouted. "They're here to overthrow you!"

Long Feng had convinced the king we were his enemies. But I told the king that I was the Avatar and he agreed to listen to me. I explained about the war and that the Dai Li had kept it secret from him in order to control the city and to control him.

"Long Feng didn't want us to tell you about all this, so he stole our sky bison to blackmail us," I explained. Now that I was finally with the king, I wasn't going to let anything stop me from telling him the truth.

Long Feng denied ever having seen a sky bison, so I Airbended his robe up to show Appa's teeth marks in his leg. Long Feng claimed it was just a birthmark, but Sokka brought Appa into the throne room and showed off his teeth.

"That pretty much proves it," the king said. "But it doesn't prove this crazy conspiracy theory," the king added.

What's it going to take to convince him that his entire kingdom is in danger?

"I suppose this matter is worth looking into," the king then said.

He agreed to come with us to give us a chance to prove that we were telling the truth. We took him to Lake Laogai to expose the Dai Li's secret headquarters, but when we got there, all evidence of the headquarters was gone. The Dai Li had already destroyed the evidence. The king was ready to return home, but then Katara had a brilliant idea.

"The wall!" she cried. "And the drill. They'll never be able to cover that up in time!"

We flew back to the city and Appa landed on top of the outer wall. The drill still stuck out of the wall, right where we stopped it.

"What is that?" the king asked anxiously.

"It's a giant drill made by the Fire Nation to break through your walls," Sokka explained.

This was proof that we were telling the truth. Now the king finally knew that the war was real.

"I can't believe I never knew," the king said.

"I can explain this, Your Majesty," said a

voice approaching us. It was Long Feng.

This ought to be good.

"This is nothing more than a construction project," he said, though it sounded as if even he had trouble believing it.

"Really?" said Katara. "Then perhaps you could explain why there's a Fire Nation insignia on your construction equipment."

I love Katara! I mean, whoa, I can't believe I admitted that, even if it is just in my own head. But I really do. I mean, she's so clever! She just backed Long Feng into a corner, and now we definitely have him right where we want him.

General Sung joined us on the wall and told the king that we were heroes.

"Without them," the general said, "our city would have been lost to the Fire Nation army."

The king ordered the Dai Li to arrest Long Feng. "He will stand trial for crimes against the Earth Kingdom," the king announced. Then the Dai Li hauled Long Feng away.

Back in the throne room, we filled in the king on the approaching comet, which would make the Fire Nation too powerful to stop, and the solar eclipse during which the Earth Kingdom army must attack the Fire Nation, which would be at its weakest. He agreed to attack on the day of the eclipse—the Day of Black Sun.

We did it! I'm so excited, I can hardly stand it! We found Appa, we saved the Earth Kingdom from the Fire Nation drill, and we delivered information to the king that can save the whole world. Sometimes it's really good being the Avatar.

Just then the door swung open and General How, leader of the council of generals, entered the throne room. He said that they'd found some things in Long Feng's office that were for us. He handed Toph a letter from her mother. Katara read it and reported that Toph's mom said she was in Ba Sing Se and wanted to see Toph.

Then he handed me a scroll.

"This scroll was attached to the horn of your bison when the Dai Li captured him," the general said.

"I can't believe it," I said after reading the note. "There's a man living at the Eastern Air Temple. A guru. A kind of spiritual expert who says he can help me take the next step in my Avatar journey."

Then he handed Katara an intelligence report that said her father was with a small fleet of Water Tribe ships at Chameleon Bay.

"I hate to say it," Katara began, "but we have to split up."

We just found Appa, and now Katara wants us to separate? I don't want to let any of them out of my sight—ever again.

"You have to meet this guru, Aang," she said. "If we're going to invade the Fire Nation, you need to be ready."

It's times like these when I wish I were just plain Aang again so that the fate of the world didn't always depend on me fulfilling my destiny. But I have no choice. She's right. I have to go.

Then Sokka pointed out that one of us had to stay there with the king and help him plan the invasion. He volunteered, but sweet, self-less Katara said that she would stay so that Sokka could go see their father.

She's the absolute best. Always putting others' needs before hers. I'm totally and completely crazy about her! There's no other way to put it. Now I just really need to tell her how I feel.

We all prepared to go our separate ways, then met up to say good-bye. I needed a moment alone with Katara, so I pulled her away from the group.

"Katara, I need to tell you something. I've been wanting to say it for a long time." Oh, boy. I'm so nervous I can hardly breathe. Here we go. . . .

"What is it, Aang?" she asked.

I've rehearsed this speech a thousand times in my head, but now that the moment is here to actually say it aloud, I don't even know where to begin. I looked up into Katara's beautiful eyes and I just blurted out—

"Katara, I—"

"All right!" Sokka shouted, punching me playfully in the stomach. "Who's ready to get going on a little men-only man trip!"

I can't believe this! Can't he see we're in the middle of something? Now the moment's gone, shattered, lost. Thanks a lot, Sokka. I was so close. . . .

Just then, a messenger arrived to tell the king that three female warriors from the island of Kyoshi were here to see him.

"That's Suki!" Sokka cried. "She'll be here
when we get back." Did I mention Sokka has a crush on Suki?

Katara, Toph, Sokka, and I stood in a circle, huddling together. Then Katara hugged me and kissed me sweetly on the head. The head's not exactly the lips, but it's a start, isn't it?

Finally, Sokka and I climbed onto Appa and off we flew. All I can think about is Katara. I miss her already and can't wait to see her face again. And from the look on Sokka's face, he's thinking about Suki.

"I can't believe I'm saying this," Sokka said. "But things are finally looking up for us."

Chapter 12

I dropped Sokka off, and Appa and I kept going till we reached the Eastern Air Temple. As we descended through the mist at sunset, I spotted a small man sitting and meditating among the overgrown gardens and ruined buildings.

He told me he was Guru Pathik, and that he could teach me how to control the Avatar state. He also said he knew my old teacher, Monk Gyatso. That's all I needed to hear. I was totally ready to learn from this guy.

Guru Pathik took me to a cave deep inside a mountain and we began. He started out by explaining that controlling the Avatar state involves finding a balance between the mind, spirit, and body. Then he explained that energy flows through the body like water in a stream, and that the body contains seven chakras. These are pools of spiraling energy. When the chakras get blocked, the energy can't flow and my power as the Avatar is weakened.

So my job is to open my seven chakras. Doesn't sound too tough!

"First we will open the Earth Chakra. It deals with survival and is blocked by fear," Guru Pathik explained.

"What are you most afraid of?" he asked. "Let your fears become clear to you."

I closed my eyes and began meditating. Visions and memories rushed into my mind—the Blue Spirit attacking me with swords, Katara being buried in rock by General Fong—and then, suddenly, Guru Pathik was gone and the Fire Lord himself was right in front of me! He filled the cave with flames.

I've failed on my first attempt! And I'm responsible for bringing the Fire Lord here to destroy the sacred temple, to kill Guru Pathik.

Then a calm voice cut through my panic

and fear. "Aang, your vision is not real."

I opened my eyes and saw Guru Pathik. No Fire Lord. No flames. It was all in my head. My hands shook and sweat poured down my face.

"You fear for your survival, but you must surrender these fears. Your spirit can never die."

"But Roku told me that if I'm killed in the Avatar state, the Avatar cycle will end!"

"Once your chakras are clear, you'll be able to control the Avatar state so that you won't need to worry about that."

Well, that makes me feel a whole lot better! Since Roku told me about the Avatar spirit, I've lived in fear of the Avatar state. I don't want to be the one to end the Avatar spirit's cycle. But since I won't have to worry about that anymore, let's try this again.

I closed my eyes and the Fire Lord stood before me.

"Let your fears flow down the creek," Guru Pathik said softly.

I don't fear you, Fire Lord. In fact, soon YOU'RE going to have to fear me. So go away. Get out of my head!

Wow! It worked. The flames in the cave are

flickering out, and the Fire Lord is vanishing into the shadows on the walls.

"You have opened your Earth Chakra."

Next came the Water Chakra, which deals with pleasure and is blocked by guilt. Again I began to meditate.

"Look at all the guilt which burdens you. What do you blame yourself for?"

My mind flooded with images of me running away from the Air Nomads when I should have stayed to complete my studies; of me screaming at Toph, blaming her when Appa was taken; and then, most powerful of all, of everyone I hurt and scared when I was out of control in the Avatar state. I hurt so many people. I don't deserve to be the Avatar.

"Accept that these things have happened, but do not let them poison your energy. If you are to be a positive influence on the world, you need to forgive yourself."

He's right. I can't change what I've done in the past, but I can try do better in the future—I hope.

"Remember how alive you felt at the moments of your greatest pleasure."

Immediately Katara's beautiful face filled

my vision and I was back in the Cave of Two Lovers. . . .

"Well, I sense that chakra just opened up like a dam!" Guru Pathik said.

Me too. I do forgive myself and I am ready to move on. I also can't wait to see Katara again!

Next came the Fire Chakra. It deals with willpower and is blocked by shame.

"What are you ashamed of? What are your biggest disappointments in yourself?" the guru asked.

I instantly saw myself struggling to learn Earthbending. Then my mind filled with my clumsy attempt at Firebending and how I burned Katara. It's clear to me now—I can't ever Firebend again. I can't risk hurting Katara or anyone else.

But when I told this to Guru Pathik, he told me I was wrong.

"You cannot deny this part of your life, Aang. You are the Avatar, and therefore you ARE a Firebender."

Right. I have to learn Firebending. There's no way around it.

I took a deep breath and pictured myself

easily controlling fire—no shame, no disappointment, just the strong will to get it right. Then I let out a burp.

"That chakra opened like a burping bison!" he remarked.

The fourth chakra was the Air Chakra. It deals with love and is blocked by grief.

Should be a piece of cake for a natural Airbender like me!

"Lay all your grief out in front of you."

Happy memories of when I was a little kid at the temple flooded my mind: when I first met Appa, when I started learning from Gyatso. Then, suddenly, Gyatso's laughing face melted into a bony skeleton. The grief bubbled up from deep inside, and tears streamed down my face.

Don't block the grief. Let it flow out.

Suddenly I was floating on a cloud in the sky surrounded by all the Air Nomads I knew growing up. They were all meditating, but as I passed each one, they disappeared. Gone, just like in real life. It was like losing them all over again. . . .

"You have indeed felt a great loss. But the love the Air Nomads had for you has not left this world. It is still inside your heart, and it is reborn in the form of new love."

There's Katara! There she is finding me frozen in the iceberg. Now it makes sense. Love never dies; it lives on inside me and makes it possible for me to love again.

The fifth chakra was the Sound Chakra. It deals with truth and is blocked by lies, the big lies we tell ourselves.

There's Katara and Sokka asking me why I didn't tell them right away that I was the Avatar. It was because I never wanted this responsibility.

"Then why do you accept it?"

It's my duty to bring balance to the world.

"Do you WANT this, or are you trying to impress someone else who thinks you SHOULD do this?"

Why is he asking me that? He's basically accusing me of not really wanting to be the Avatar. But I do want to be the Avatar! I think.

The visions of Katara and Sokka melted from my mind, and I was suddenly alone on a high mountaintop. I looked out at the world.

I do like being the Avatar. I WANT this. I know that now. The world is depending on me, and that's okay.

"Very good, Aang. You have opened your Sound Chakra to truth."

The sixth chakra was the Light Chakra. It deals with insight and is blocked by illusion. Guru Pathik explained that the big illusion is the illusion of separation. People are connected. So are the four nations. We are all one people. In fact, even the separation of the four elements is an illusion.

I opened my mind and saw an image of the four elements blending. Then the vision shifted to Toph Earthbending metal. I get it! The four elements are just four parts of the same whole. Even metal is just earth that has been changed into a different form. Just then the Light Chakra opened for me. One more to go.

"Once you open the final chakra, you'll be able to move in and out of the Avatar state at will. And you will have complete control and awareness of all your actions while in the Avatar state."

I am so psyched! This is why I came here. This is the big step that will allow me to defeat the Fire Lord and unite the world. Let's go. I'm ready!

The guru told me that the Thought Chakra deals with pure cosmic energy and is blocked by all earthly attachments.

"To begin, Aang, you must meditate on what attaches you to this world."

Instantly my mind filled with thoughts of Katara. I saw us together in all the things we've been through, and I realized that I'm never happier than when I'm with her.

"Now, let all of these attachments go," he continued. "Let them flow away, forgotten. . . . Learn to let her go, or you cannot let pure cosmic energy flow in from the universe."

What? What's he talking about? Why would I ever want to let go of Katara? I love her. This must be some kind of mistake. How can feeling an attachment to Katara be a bad thing? She means everything to me. I don't understand—and just when I thought this was going to be easy.

"I'm sorry, but I can't let go of Katara."

"Aang, you must clear all the chakras to master the Avatar state. The Thought Chakra is your gate to all the energy in the universe. You must trust it and surrender yourself."

I closed my eyes again, trying to let go. I saw myself walking on a narrow bridge over the universe. Katara was there with me on the bridge, but as I relaxed, she lifted into the sky, growing smaller and smaller until she became just one more glowing star in the cosmos. I turned around and saw this giant standing at the end of the bridge.

Wait. That giant is me, in the Avatar state. I get it now! I have to reach myself in the Avatar state to clear the Thought Chakra.

I walked toward the giant, but then, suddenly, I heard Katara screaming. I spun around and saw her bound in chains, locked in a prison.

Katara's in trouble. I'm certain of it. I have to save her.

But the giant Avatar also beckoned me.

What am I supposed to do? Do I continue to cleanse the final chakra and let go of Katara? Can I give up the person I love most in the world, or do I turn my back on learning to control the Avatar state? I can't just ignore her! What if she's in real danger?

I turned away from the giant Avatar and ran across the bridge to where Katara was trapped, but the bridge crumbled beneath my feet and I fell into the vast emptiness of space, lost forever.

Then I opened my eyes. I was back with Guru Pathik. I jumped to my feet in a panic.

"Katara is in danger. I have to go!"

Guru Pathik told me that by choosing Katara, I had locked the last chakra.

"Aang, if you leave now, you won't be able to go into the Avatar state at all!"

Somewhere in a distant corner of my mind, a voice is telling me to stay and complete my journey. Sorry, voice, Katara's in trouble. I could never live with myself if anything happened to her that I could have prevented. I don't want to lose the power of the Avatar state, but if being the Avatar means that I have to give up everyone I love, maybe I don't want to be the Avatar after all. Isn't the Avatar SUPPOSED to do things like help people in danger? Maybe THIS is what I'm meant to do BECAUSE I'm the Avatar. Either way, I know I need to save Katara because I'm Aang. I have no choice.

I leaped onto Appa's back and took off for Ba Sing Se as fast as I could.

Chapter 13

On the way back to the city, I stopped and picked up Sokka. Then we spotted Toph below, surfing a wave of earth. Appa swooped down and we picked her up too. Sokka told us about how great it was to see his dad, and Toph told us that she learned how to bend metal! First I just thought, Gosh, she's such an amazing Earthbender. But then I thought about my visions with the guru, and how I'd seen Toph bending metal in one of them when I was trying to cleanse the Light Chakra. The Light Chakra is blocked by illusions, and just like the Waterbender from the swamp and the guru told me, time really must be an illusion, because the vision I saw in the swamp of Toph laughing and the vision I saw just a while ago of her bending metal both came true!

And all of this means that my vision of Katara must be real—she must really be in danger! It also probably means that the guru is right—my seventh chakra is blocked. Well, first things first, I guess. Both Toph and Sokka were upset when I told them about the vision of Katara, and we sped off for Ba Sing Se as quickly as Appa could take us there.

They asked me how my experience with the guru went. I lied to them and told them I com—pletely mastered the Avatar state. As much as they love Katara, they won't understand my choice. They'll think I abandoned my responsi—bility. And maybe I did. I don't know. But what I do know is that I have to make sure Katara is okay. I also know that I had to lie about this. I don't feel good about it, but I can't deal with all this now. First Katara, then I'll figure out how to make all the Avatar stuff right—I hope.

We landed in Ba Sing Se and hurried to the king's throne room. But to my surprise he told me that Katara was off with the Kyoshi warriors and doing fine. We headed for our apartment, where I was greeted by Momo—but no Katara.

She IS in trouble. I knew it. My vision was right.

Then a knock came at the door. Toph threw open the door and there stood Zuko's uncle, Iroh!

This is the last thing I need, to battle Iroh. Is Zuko with him? Maybe they have Katara. . . .

It turned out that Toph and Iroh had met before, in the woods when Toph ran away from us, and they'd become friends.

"Toph, I need your help," Iroh said. "Princess Azula is in Ba Sing Se."

Azula! SHE must have Katara. Now I'm really worried. Azula nearly killed me the last time we fought. She's crazy, and super dangerous. How are we going to save Katara?

Iroh explained that Azula had captured Katara and Zuko.

"We'll work together to fight Azula and save Zuko and Katara," I said.

Sokka was shocked when I said we'd rescue Zuko. I guess I was a bit surprised myself. But I'm willing to do anything to save Katara, and after dealing with Azula, Zuko really didn't seem so bad.

Iroh brought along a Dai Li agent he had captured. The agent told us that Azula and Long Feng were plotting to overthrow the Earth King! He also said that Katara was being held in the crystal catacombs of old Ba Sing Se, deep beneath the palace.

Toph Earthbended a tunnel beneath the palace, then we split up. While Sokka and Toph went to warn the Earth King about Azula's coup, Iroh and I headed into the tunnel to rescue Katara and Zuko.

First I started actually feeling sorry for Zuko, now I'm trusting his uncle, a retired Fire Nation general. Boy, it's strange how things change. You think you have stuff all fig-ured out, who's good and who's evil, and then people go and surprise you.

Toph's tunnel led us into a crystal courtyard, a wide-open plaza with waterfalls and a stream running over beautiful crystal rocks. I used Earth-bending to open sections of the courtyard's walls until I finally found Katara's and Zuko's prison.

"Aang! I knew you would come!" Katara rushed over and hugged me.

Thank goodness she's okay! Now I know I made the right choice.

Just then Zuko rushed at me, but Iroh stopped him. Those two had a lot to talk about, so Katara and I left them and headed off to find Sokka and Toph.

But before we got out of the crystal court-yard, Azula attacked! She fired bolts of blue lightning. Katara countered by Waterbending water from the stream as I used Earthbending to block Azula's blasts and knock her off balance.

Azula may be too much for me alone, but working with Katara, I think I'm going to beat her. Wait, Zuko's back! Did his uncle convince him to help us or will he join Azula against us? I wonder what he'll choo—

BAM!

Zuko just sent a fire blast headed right at me! So much for people surprising me. Same old Zuko. Only now he's teamed with his ruthless sis-ter! I hope we have what it takes to beat them. . . .

Oh, no! Katara's hurt. She just fell down into the stream. . . . Azula must have zapped her as she stepped into the water, shocking her! I didn't save her! I rejected Guru Pathik to save her and I still failed.

Now a troop of Dai Li agents are joining in the fight, throwing Earthbending attacks at me. There are too many of them. I can't stop them all AND beat Azula and Zuko.

Guru Pathik is right. I'm holding on to my earthly attachment and ruining everything. There's only one way to make this better: I have to let her go.

I'm sorry, Katara.

I Earthbended a protective crystal shell around myself, and then I began to meditate.

I'm back on that bridge, walking toward the giant version of myself in the Avatar state. . . .

Don't hesitate this time; just walk toward the giant Aang. Accept your fate. . . .

It's working! I'm slipping into the Avatar state! I feel more powerful than I ever have before!

BOOM!

What's that? What hit me? Oh, no. The bridge, it's crumbling beneath my feet. . . . I'm falling. . . .

I could hear Katara's voice drifting softly through the darkness. Then I felt myself slowly waking up. In my mind I saw a glowing band of golden water soothing me, restoring me.

When I finally opened my eyes, I was stretched out on Appa's back, flying away from Ba Sing Se. Katara kneeled over me, healing me with her Waterbending. I hugged her and we both started to cry. She told me that Iroh had helped us escape. I guess some people will still surprise me after all.

When I sat up, I saw that Sokka, Toph, and the Earth King were with us. The Earth King looked down at the city and sighed.

"The Earth Kingdom has fallen," he said solemnly.

Everything was my fault—again. What if I had made a different choice? What if I had been able to give up Katara the first time, cleansed my chakra, and gained control of the Avatar state? Maybe the Earth Kingdom would now be free. Maybe Azula and Zuko would be defeated. Maybe the war would be over.

But it isn't. I have to find a way to make all this right. I just hope I can find the strength to figure out how. . . .

降去神通

AVATAR
THE LAST AIRBENDER

THE EARTH KINGDOM CHRONICLES:
THE TALE OF
AZULA

by Michael Teitelbaum
based on original screenplays
written for *Avatar: The Last Airbender*

SIMON SPOTLIGHT/NICKELODEON
New York London Toronto Sydney

Chapter 1

My name is Azula. I am a princess of the Fire Nation. My father is Fire Lord Ozai, leader of the most powerful nation on Earth. Soon he will rule all the nations—Fire, Earth, Water, and Air. They will fall under his iron grip once my work is complete. Then, in time, I will succeed my father to the throne of the Fire Nation and become the next Fire Lord.

But first things first. My task at the moment is to track down my uncle and my brother and return them to the Fire Lord for the punishment they deserve. My uncle Iroh is a traitor and a coward. Oh sure, once he was considered a great warrior, but when he ran from the battle of Ba Sing Se, he let control of the Earth Kingdom slip from his grasp. For that he has been banished from the Fire Nation for life.

And what of my beloved big brother, Zuko? He is a failure, total and complete. My father said so just recently when he assigned me this task. Of course I already knew: Zuko's been insufferable since we were children—a weak, whiny boy who never actually grew up. Whenever things didn't go his way, he would go crying to our mother—until one day she was no longer there to protect him. He would never stand up for himself, and he certainly never stood up to me. He's been afraid of me since I was nine years old, and that's just the way I like it. I'm fourteen now, and I could destroy him with just one look. And to think that he's next in line to become Fire Lord! The very idea makes me laugh.

I know Zuko's older than me. But Iroh is older than HIS brother, and Iroh's cowardice and incompetence rendered him unworthy of the throne. And so it was my father, Ozai, who became Fire Lord. Well, history has a strange way of repeating itself. I believe that once again the younger sibling will ascend to the throne of the Fire Nation when the time comes. I will be the next Fire Lord, definitely not my useless brother.

Zuko was banished from the Fire Nation for disrespecting our father. He has since been searching for the Avatar, to bring that little pest back to Father and eliminate any threat to the Fire Nation's plan for world domination. But, of course, Zuko has failed. Time and again the Avatar has slipped through his fingers, and Zuko now runs and hides in disgrace with our uncle. But he cannot run forever, and he certainly cannot run from me!

My father has supplied me with a beautiful ship, a Fire Nation royal sloop, to be precise—and I am nothing if not precise. The ship is filled with the luxuries befitting a princess, and is crewed by Fire Nation soldiers at my command. A great warrior and leader deserves nothing less.

As the magnificent ship approached the port where Iroh and Zuko had last been seen, I addressed the troops who gathered on deck.

"My brother and uncle have disgraced the Fire Lord and brought shame on all of us. I understand that you may have mixed feelings about attacking members of the royal family, but I assure you, if you hesitate in your duty to me and to your country, I will not hesitate to bring you down."

I can feel the fear spreading among them like a plague. Good. I like it when people are afraid of me. Frightened soldiers are obedient soldiers. They will obey my every wish, or they will know my wrath. Trust me. They don't want to know my wrath.

"Dismissed!"

As the troops hurried off to their posts, the ship's captain, a spineless little weasel, came scurrying up to me, muttering some gibberish about how the tides wouldn't allow him to bring the ship into port before nightfall.

I know just how to handle this poor excuse for a soldier. "I'm sorry, Captain," I said with extreme politeness, "but I do not know much about the tides. Can you explain something to me?"

"Of course, Your Highness."

Weakling. I'd love to get rid of him. But then who would steer the ship? "Do the tides command this ship?" I asked him.

"I'm afraid I don't understand."

Of course you don't. You have no idea how close you are to vanishing in a flash of blue flame. "You said the tides would not allow us to bring the ship in. So again I ask you: Do the tides command this ship?"

"No, Princess."

He seems to be catching on. Good. "And if I were to have you thrown overboard, would the tides think twice about smashing you against the rocky shore?"

"No, Princess."

I see the sweat bead on his forehead and his neck muscles tighten. He is afraid of me. "Well then, Captain, maybe you should worry less about the tides, who've already made up their mind about killing you, and worry more about me, who's still mulling it over."

At this point the nervous man won't even make eye contact with me. "I—I'll p—pull us in at once, Your Highness," he stammered, swallowing hard.

Smart man. I'll let you live. For today, anyway.

⊕ ⊕ ⊕

Once we docked I made my way to a resort where our intelligence indicated that Iroh and Zuko were hiding out. Ha! Do they really think they can hide from the Fire Lord, or from me?

As I approached their thatched hut on the beach, my stomach turned. Fugitives hiding out in luxury—how perfect.

I moved silently to the hut, then peered through its window. There was Iroh, beaming with pride over his worthless collection of seashells. This was the once great warrior of the Fire Nation? The "Dragon of the West"? What a joke!

And there was my sweet brother, throwing a temper tantrum because he had to carry his own bags. Poor little prince: so spoiled, so pitiful. But kind Azula has a surprise for you both.

"Hello, Brother; Uncle," I said, stepping into their hut.

"What are YOU doing here?" Zuko cried, moving swiftly into an attack pose.

My, my, what a brave warrior, ready to defend his vacation hut. But so rude! Zu-zu needs to be taught a lesson in manners. Zu-zu. He hates it when I call him that. "In MY country we exchange a pleasant 'hello' before asking questions," I said. "Have you become so uncivilized so soon, Zu-zu?"

"Don't call me that!"

So predictable, my brother.

"To what do we owe this honor?" Iroh asked coldly.

Zuko masked his fear with bluster, Iroh with his stoic manner. But I know they both fear me. As well they should. "Must be a family trait— both of you so quick to get to the point," I said. "I've come with a message from home: Zuko, Father's changed his mind. Family is suddenly very important to him. He's heard rumors of plans to overthrow him—treacherous plots."

I think Zuko is intrigued by my "news," but he's showing me nothing of what he feels.

This next bit should get him, though. "Family are the only ones you can really trust," I told him in my most sincere tone. "So what I've come to tell you is this: Father regrets your banishment. He wants you to come home."

I'm still not getting a reaction from Zuko. Is he trying hard to be brave, or is he just stupid?

"Did you hear me?" I asked impatiently. "You should be happy. Excited. Grateful. I just gave you great news!"

"I am sure your brother simply needs a moment to—"

"Don't interrupt, Uncle!" I snapped. "I still haven't heard my thank-you. I'm not a messenger. I didn't have to come all this way to deliver the good news."

Zuko's eyes are glazed over. I believe he heard me, but he looks as if he's stunned. I admit I must have caught him off guard, but—

"Father . . . regrets . . . he wants me back?"

Ah, there's the hope and relief I was looking for. The fish has taken the bait. Why did I even think this would be a difficult task?

He is clearly mine. Now I just have to finish playing my role. "I can see you need time to take this in," I said. "I'll come to call on you tomorrow. Good evening."

I left the hut and hurried back to my ship. There is much to be done to prepare for my dear brother's return. After all, it's not every day that the prince of the Fire Nation boards a ship heading home for a "hero's welcome"!

🔆 🔆 🔆

The next morning all was ready. I lined my soldiers up on deck. They have their orders, and each one had better follow them to the letter. I'm waiting in my quarters. Is it possible they won't show? I don't think Zuko can resist the idea that Father has forgiven him, but I can't be too sure just yet of what he will do.

At that moment, one of my soldiers knocked on the door to tell me that Zuko and Iroh were approaching the ship. I hurried up to the deck.

As Zuko and Iroh stepped onto the gangplank leading up to the ship, I flashed them a big smile. "Brother! Uncle! Welcome!"

They are here. This is all too easy. "I'm so glad you decided to come!"

As Zuko stepped onto the deck I gave him a big hug. Then I bowed oh-so-respectfully to Iroh. That's when the captain stepped up to me and asked if we were ready to depart.

"Set our course for home, Captain."

Once again Zuko's eyes glazed over, lost in dreams of his homecoming. "Home," he mumbled to himself.

The captain turned to his crew. "You heard the princess!" he shouted. "Raise the anchors! We're taking the prisoners home—" The captain suddenly stopped, realizing his mistake.

PRISONERS! You incompetent fool!

Iroh looked at me with daggers in his eyes. He didn't trust me from the start, and now he knows the truth. But Zuko is so in love with the idea of going home that he still hasn't realized the meaning of the captain's words.

The captain turned toward me, looking for understanding and forgiveness. "Your highness, I—I—"

But I ignored him. Right now I have a more

immediate situation to take care of.

"Run!" Iroh shouted. My uncle sent a few of my soldiers overboard with some Firebending.

But poor, deluded Zuko couldn't believe his little sister had betrayed him. He charged right at me, rage burning in his eyes. "You lied to me!" he shouted.

How can you be so naive, big brother? Always expecting people to behave the way you would like them to behave instead of looking at the world the way it really is. "Like I've never done that before," I said smugly.

He really should know me by now. Oh, he's so angry! He may actually get up the nerve to attack me.

And he did. Zuko threw all he had at me, unleashing a Firebending barrage. Impressive, but nothing I couldn't handle. He's far too emotional and unfocused. I easily sidestepped or blocked each of his feeble attacks. I saw no need to strike back . . . yet.

First I'll just have some fun.

"You know Father blames Iroh for the loss at the North Pole," I taunted.

Oh, Zuko is furious! How delightful! His feeble attacks amuse me, and I can't resist continuing. "And he considers you a miserable failure for not finding the Avatar."

That one's sending him over the edge! He's even trying to kick me, just like when we were little. And just as I was then, I'm faster and better than he is. I'd almost forgotten how much fun this is.

"Why would Father want you back home, except to lock you up where you can no longer embarrass him?" I said with a smile on my face.

Look at him, screaming with all his helpless fury. There! He's overextended himself. Time to end this little charade.

I struck him with a series of swift Firebending jabs, far too fast for him to defend himself. Then I drove him back to the deck, where he lay sprawled, powerless to stop me. Now I will end this with a blast of lightning!

But as I unleashed a powerful bolt of blue lightning, Iroh redirected the blast away from Zuko and the ship. The lightning bolt slammed into a nearby mountain. THOOM! The force of the blast caused the deck to explode into a thousand fragments, and sent me flying off the ship and into the water.

Iroh! I should have gotten rid of him immediately when I saw him yesterday. Father surely would not have mourned the loss of such a traitor and coward.

My soldiers dove from the burning ship to save me, but I did not require saving. "Forget about me, you fools," I told them. "I am perfectly capable of swimming to safety! Go stop Iroh and Zuko!"

But they were too late. By the time the soldiers swam back to the ship, my tiresome brother and uncle were gone. I have failed in my first attempt to capture them. But no matter. First my incompetent crew will pay dearly for this disaster, and then I will resume my search. I will bring those two back to Father. Of that I have no doubt—but perhaps I need a different strategy for my next step.

Chapter 2

After returning to what was left of my ship, I ordered my soldiers to round up everyone who worked at the resort. I should destroy them all for giving Iroh and Zuko a safe place to hide, but I will hold off for now. They may come in handy, especially if I offer a little added incentive.

I created a poster with images of Iroh and Zuko. Then I stepped from the ship and addressed the gathered employees of the resort, holding the poster high above my head.

"Anyone who harbors these two traitors will face the wrath of the Fire Lord!" I announced, rattling the poster for extra effect.

The crowd let out a gasp. Good, just the kind of reaction I wanted. They fear me and they fear Father. It is now only a matter of time before the fugitives are firmly in my grasp.

I consulted with my advisers, two wise old women, Lo and Li. They sat in lotus positions on either side of me as I contemplated my next move.

"When tracking your brother and uncle, traveling with the royal procession may no longer be an option," Lo stated.

"It may no longer be wise," Li added.

"If you hope to keep the element of surprise," Lo and Li said together.

Wise words indeed. The pomp and grandeur of this huge ship, this royal procession with all its luxurious trappings, are my birthright. But in this case they may serve as an early warning signal to

Zuko and Iroh that I am close at hand. Two individuals traveling light will have stealth, secrecy, and speed on their side against all this dead weight.

If I want to catch my prey I must be agile and nimble. I must change my approach. I will leave all this behind. I need to enlist the help of a small, fast, elite team of operatives whom I trust completely. We will move swiftly and silently, and trap the fugitives when they least expect it.

It's time I visit some old friends and recruit

them to this all—important task.

🔆 🔆 🔆

My first stop in the search for my team was a circus. I was looking for an old friend from childhood.

Ah, there she is. It's been years since I've seen her, but she looks the same. Slim, athletic, and full of energy. She is working as an acrobat in the circus. What a dreadful waste of her talent—it is a disgusting, unpleasant place. What could she possibly see in all this filth? But it doesn't really matter. The next phase of her life, in which she serves her nation and her Fire Lord, is about to begin. I am sure of it.

"Ty Lee, could that possibly be you?" I ask politely, knowing the answer.

She turned and looked right at me. "Azula!" Ty Lee exclaimed excitedly. Then she untwisted herself out of the pretzel-like pose she had been in, and bowed respectfully to me. Even though we are old friends, it is good that she knows her place—and that she realizes exactly who she is dealing with. "It's so good to see you, Azula!"

"Please don't let me interrupt your . . . whatever it is you're doing," I said, glad that she was so enthusiastic to see me. She will prove to be a valuable ally.

Ty Lee went back to her stretching as I wondered what she was doing here among the smelly animals and circus performers. She is, after all, the daughter of a nobleman, and she attended the Royal Fire Academy for Girls, just as I did. I'm certain her parents would not want her to end up in a horrid place like this.

"Ty Lee, I have a proposition for you," I said. "I'm hunting a traitor. You remember my old fuddy-duddy uncle, don't you?"

"Oh yeah, he was so funny!"

Funny! What could she possibly find funny about that pathetic old man? My face tightened.

Sensing my displeasure, Ty Lee quickly and nervously added, "I mean, what a shame he's become a traitor."

Good. She knows when she's crossed the line with me. "I would be honored if you would join me on my mission," I continued.

"Oh, I would love to, really," Ty Lee replied. "But the truth is, I'm really happy here. I love this life."

I was not expecting her to say this at all, but I don't show my surprise. Her mind will change soon enough. "Well, I wouldn't want you to give up the life you love just to please me," I said, knowing that she eventually would.

Ty Lee bowed. "Thank you, Azula," she said respectfully.

"Of course, before I leave, I'm going to catch your show," I said sweetly.

"Um, yeah, sure, of course," said Ty Lee, as a look of confusion crossed her face.

Later that evening I entered the circus tent for Ty Lee's performance. I was shown to a private area, and was seated in an elaborate chair that resembled a throne. Proper respect for the princess of the Fire Nation. I was pleased to see it.

The circus master came hurrying over to me and bowed. "We are deeply honored to have the Fire Lord's daughter at our humble circus. Please tell us if there is anything we can do to make the show more enjoyable."

"I will," I replied.

I watched Ty Lee perform with confidence, high up on a tightrope. With the palm of one hand planted on a board that was balanced on a cylinder, she lifted her body straight up, her toes pointing toward the top of the tent. It is good to know her remarkable skills have not dulled with time. If anything, they have improved. "Incredible!" I exclaimed to the circus master. "Do you think she'll fall?"

"Of course not," he replied, without taking his attention away from Ty Lee.

"Then wouldn't it make things more

interesting if you removed the net?"

He looked at me, obviously shocked by the suggestion. But I could see that this useless circus person would not dare to defy my will. I could up the ante a bit more. "I know! Set the net on fire."

He was too afraid to disagree. With a quick Firebending blast, he set the safety net ablaze. Ty Lee, the dear, kept her balance, but I could see the sweat bead on her forehead. I hope she's beginning to get my point—but perhaps I could make it a bit clearer. "What kind of dangerous animals do you have?"

"Well, Princess," he began, "our circus boasts the most exotic assortment of—"

"Release them all!" I commanded.

The expression of horror on the man's face was absolutely priceless! He bowed, then hurried away. A few seconds later a thundering herd of animals charged from the back of the tent. Ty Lee's tightrope shook. She teetered on the brink of disaster, but, trooper that she is, she kept her balance. I see more sweat than before. Excellent. Perhaps my point has been made. If not, I'll just have to endure another performance.

After the show I joined Ty Lee in her dressing room. She noticed me walking in, but did not acknowledge my presence. Her face revealed nothing, but I knew that she was afraid. She remained silent. It was up to me to draw a response.

"What an exquisite performance, Ty Lee," I said admiringly. "In fact, I've decided to stay in town. I can't wait to see how you'll top yourself tomorrow night."

That did it. She turned and faced me. "I'm sorry, Azula," she said, smiling. "Unfortunately there won't be a show tomorrow."

You are good, I told myself. All it took was a few minutes and a few simple suggestions. "Really?" I asked, trying to sound genuinely surprised.

"The universe is giving me strong hints that it's time for a career change," she replied sweetly. "I want to join you on your mission!"

That was nice and easy. The first piece of the puzzle has fallen into place, and now it's on to Omashu for the next step in my plan.

Ty Lee and I journeyed to Omashu, the former Earth Kingdom city that now belongs to the Fire Nation. We were there to see another childhood friend, Mai, who just happens to be the daughter of Omashu's Fire Nation governor.

We met in front of the governor's palace, where Mai greeted me with a formal bow. It is good to see that she, too, does not take our early friendship for granted, and that she is wise enough to show me the respect I deserve.

"PLEASE tell me that you're here to kill me," Mai said dramatically. "Omashu is the most boring place in the world."

Then we both laughed and hugged. I've always appreciated her sense of humor, along with her loyalty. "It's great to see you, Mai," I said.

"I thought you ran off and joined the circus, Ty Lee," Mai said. "You said it was your calling."

"Well, Azula called a little louder," Ty Lee replied.

Good girl. I see her loyalty is also beyond doubt. "I have a mission and I need you both,"

I told Mai. And without any hesitation, she responded, "Count me in!"

This was excellent. Mai didn't even need to hear what the mission was. I now have two underlings who will obey me without question, who will fight and give their lives for me if necessary. Iroh and Zuko are practically in my hands.

"Just get me out of this place," Mai added. "I'm DYING for some excitement."

Soon you will have more excitement than you can imagine, my friend. But I must take care of one small piece of business first.

🟦 🟦 🟦

I had Ty Lee and Mai wait outside while I visited the governor in his throne room. Mai briefed me on the recent happenings in Omashu, and I am not pleased. Granted, the former king of Omashu, Bumi, is now a prisoner since he surrendered the Fire Nation, but apparently her incompetent father has simply allowed most of the citizens to just walk out of the city. It's inconceivable to me how he could let that happen! Among them was his young son, who ended up in the hands of the resistance. And now the leaders of the resistance want to trade the former king for the governor's son.

"I apologize, Princess," the governor said. "You have come to Omashu at a difficult time. At noon we're making a trade with the resistance to get my son back."

You're trading a king—an Earth Kingdom leader—for a toddler? I hate sentimental drivel. "Yes, I'm sorry to hear about your son," I said, not feeling sorry at all. "But really, what did you expect by just letting all the citizens leave?"

"We thought there was a dangerous plague spreading," the governor replied. "We didn't know it was a trick."

I could not believe he was actually admitting how stupid he was! How did he become governor?

"My father has trusted you with this city and you're making a mess of things!" I snapped. "And in case you haven't heard, my father is not a very forgiving man!"

"Forgive me, Princess," the governor said nervously. "I CAN govern Omashu. I WILL do better. I just need a little time."

Time is a luxury you do not have. "You stay here. Mai will handle the hostage trade so you don't mess it up. And I will be by her side."

"Thank you, Princess."

Don't thank me too quickly. I will deal with you in due time.

Ty Lee, Mai, and I approached a wide plaza near the top of the city. Mai had handled the preparations for the return of King Bumi. All was ready.

A delegation of three resistance fighters approached us from the far end of the plaza: a short boy wearing a turban and carrying a staff, a girl, and a taller boy who carried the governor's child. I let a moment pass, then nodded for Mai to begin.

At a signal from Mai, a crane lowered a large metal cage from above. King Bumi peered wildly through a small window. This is the great Earth Kingdom king? He looks like a giggling lunatic who deserves to be locked up. Still, he is a king, and obviously of great importance to these people.

Mai stepped forward, as did the rebel with the turban.

"You brought my younger brother," she said.

"We're ready to trade," the boy replied.

Mai nodded. *But something is not right about this. It's too easy, and we're giving up far too much. I refuse to let this happen. Still, this is Mai's little brother we're talking about. I must depend on her unwavering loyalty to me—which will now be tested for the first time.*

I leaned toward Mai and spoke softly. "I'm sorry, but a thought just occurred to me. Do you mind?"

"Of course not, Princess Azula. What is it?"

The respect and fear is in her voice, and she addresses me by my formal title. This may not be much of a problem. "We're trading a two-year-old for a king," I explained. "A powerful Earthbending king at that. It just doesn't seem like a fair trade, does it?"

Now it's up to Mai. Will she agree with

me blindly, putting aside any feelings she has for her brother, or will this be the first conflict in our new alliance? She looked at me, expressionless, then glanced over at her brother, who was squirming in the arms of the taller boy. Then she looked back at me.

"You're right," she said. Then she raised her voice and called out, "The deal's off!" She signaled with her hand, and the crane lifted King Bumi's metal container back up into the air.

Excellent! You will be rewarded for your loyalty, my old friend.

"Whooah!" King Bumi shouted as his cage rose skyward. "See you all later!"

The boy with the turban raced toward the crane. "Bumi, no!" he shouted.

So this resistance fighter has decided to be a hero. I will show him that he has made a grave error in judgment.

I unleashed a wall of blue flame blocking his way. But then something amazing happened: The boy leaped into the air, and his staff opened into an Airbender's glider! Then his turban blew off in the wind, revealing an arrow—shaped tattoo on his bald head. He is the Avatar!

Well, well, well. This IS my lucky day! It appears that I'm going to get much more than a toddler out of this deal. The taller boy and the girl had taken off with the little runt, but Mai and Ty Lee are sure to catch them.

Today I will succeed where my pathetic brother has failed so often. Today I will capture the Avatar!

The Avatar flew up and landed on Bumi's box. Then, using his breath, and what appeared to be a form of Waterbending, he began freezing the metal chain that held it up.

But he will not complete this task. Using the pulley system that had lowered the cage, I hoisted myself up above the Avatar, then shot a burst of fire right at him.

No! My fire burst has only served to snap the chain and release Bumi's box, with the Avatar still on top of it. It's plummeting toward the city's mail chutes. Wait—my plan may succeed after all. When the container slams into that chute, both Bumi and the Avatar will be destroyed in one swift stroke!

Uh—oh. The Avatar has created some kind of air cushion to soften their landing. Clever. You are quite the challenge, Avatar.

I jumped into a cart used to carry mail along the chutes, and set off after them. I fired a blast, but the Avatar simply spun his staff, creating a whirlwind that redirected my fire burst.

Oh, this is taking much longer than necessary. I unleashed a barrage of fireballs one after another, but again the Avatar proved resourceful, outrunning or dodging my—

What's this? The Avatar has used his Airbending power to slice off the tops of the metal support beams above the mail chute! The beams have tumbled onto the track. I'm going to crash! I have to time this perfectly.

I leaped high into the air as my cart bounced through the rubble on the track. When it righted itself, I landed gently in the cart and continued my pursuit. Suddenly an enormous flying creature of some kind appeared out of nowhere. From the looks of it, it was a huge white bison. I have heard about Airbenders and their companion bison—this must belong to the Avatar. He's trying to make his escape. If he reaches the bison, I'll never catch up!

As I fired another burst of blue-hot flame, the Avatar lifted Bumi's box up off the track and soared toward the bison. Ah! He's overshot his target. They are flying right over the creature, and they're still in the chute.

I have to think fast. No one has ever resisted my fire-pinwheel attack, so I spun my hands swiftly, creating a rotating pinwheel of searing flames, then launched it at the container. This will put an end to—

Ahhh! A wall of rock rose up through the track, blocking my pinwheel blast. In a matter of seconds I'll crash right into the rock! I jumped out of the mail cart, which smashed into bits against the rock wall. Landing on the tracks, I could only watch helplessly, my fury growing, as Bumi and the Avatar escaped.

This boy is skillful and resourceful. But he has no idea with whom he is tangling. It is only a matter of time before he is mine.

I returned to the palace, where Ty Lee and Mai were waiting after chasing the other resistance fighters for a while. As we prepared to leave I explained our mission to them.

"So we're tracking down your brother and uncle, huh?" Mai asked.

Ty Lee couldn't resist the chance to tease Mai. "It'll be interesting to see Zuko again, won't it, Mai?"

They both laughed. When we were kids, Mai had a crush on Zuko. He may have felt the same way, but he was so busy brooding and sulking all the time there was no way to really tell.

I told the girls that our mission had changed somewhat. Though Father charged me with the task of bringing Zuko and Iroh back to him, I have now set my sights on a third target as well. Not only will I fulfill Father's wishes, but I will also deliver the biggest prize of all, the one that has eluded my brother: the Avatar!

降击神通

Chapter 3

Tracking the Avatar is proving to be a more difficult task than I expected. His flying bison gives him an advantage, as he is free to travel anywhere without concern for roads, mountains, lakes, or other obstacles. We followed the Avatar through as much of the Earth Kingdom as we could cover, but soon lost him in the rugged terrain. I knew I needed a vehicle that could handle any environment I encountered. I acquired the finest all—terrain vehicle in the Fire Nation. It was a huge ironclad tank, with three sharp spikes that jutted out from the front. A tall smokestack belched black fumes from its top, and the thick treads of the tires were designed to travel over rock, sand, and water. The vehicle was even capable of climbing straight up the sides of mountains! Powered by fire itself, this tank could go forever without running out of fuel. Also traveling with us were three agile mongoose-dragons. We were more than ready for our pursuit of the Avatar.

We began our hunt and found that luck was on our side. A short distance from Omashu, we discovered several large clumps of thick, white fur leading in a straight line toward the mountains.

I recognize this fur. It is the fur of the Avatar's bison! Perhaps this is a sign, telling me that it won't be long before I stand before my father with the Avatar at my side.

Energized by this finding, I poured more fire into the tank's engine to increase our speed. With the city far behind us, we encountered a long, flat plain that stretched out for miles, leading to the mountains in the distance. There, in a wooded area at the edge of the plain, blue smoke curled into the sky.

I've found them!

I pushed the machine even harder, picking up speed. A short while later we reached the remains of a campsite at the edge of the woods. Charred cinders from a campfire that had been doused in water smoked and sizzled. Impressions in the grass showed where tents and bedrolls had been set up.

We are too late! They must have known we were coming and fled. But how? How could they know we were following them?

Then I noticed an odd tent, made from rock, jutting out of the earth. Is the Avatar now an Earthbender too? Or did one of his party do this? Perhaps whoever created this tent could sense the vibrations of our tank rumbling through the ground. I have heard that some Earthbenders can do that. But they cannot run forever, especially not from me.

We followed the trail of fur deeper into the woods. Our tank simply flattened smaller trees, while I steered around the larger ones. As we approached a clearing in the woods, there was a flash of movement. Several people rushed around in a panic, and then I saw them—the Avatar's bison rising into the sky, with four figures mounted on its back.

They headed deep into the mountains. The Avatar must think he can lose me, but he does not realize that his bison is leaving a convenient trail of fur. And of course, he has no idea what this Fire Nation tank is capable of.

We arrived at the base of a tall mountain, and then began to climb—straight up! We were amazed at how easily the tank did this. When we reached a plateau, there stood the Avatar and three others.

Apparently they were waiting for us— and ready to fight. Well, that's exactly what we were ready to do as well.

"Prepare the animals for battle!" I ordered. I shut down the tank's engine, and the tank rolled to a stop. Then Ty Lee, Mai, and I mounted the mongoose-dragons that had traveled with us. "Ready, girls? Now the fun begins!"

I threw open the door of the tank and we charged toward our enemies, riding the lizards hard. When we came to a river the creatures reared back, splashing across the water on their hind legs, their colorful necks flared wide open. Once back on solid ground, they dropped down to all fours and picked up speed.

Suddenly a jagged mound of rock sprang from the earth right in front of me. I tugged my reins hard to the left and skipped around the obstacle, but another quickly appeared before me. Again and again, rocks rose in my path, and in front of Ty Lee and Mai as well. However, mongoose–dragons are very swift and nimble creatures, and they were able to maneuver around each rock.

But who was responsible for creating these obstacles? I looked around as I pulled on the reins of my mongoose–dragon. That's when I saw a girl who had not been with the Avatar and his two companions at the exchange in Omashu. She stomped her foot on the ground, and a huge wall of rock exploded from the earth in front of me.

So the Avatar has found a skilled Earthbender to help him. Cute of him to think that I could be stopped by someone like her. But this is getting tiresome, and I don't plan on going around any more of these rocks. The time has come to go THROUGH them.

I fired a powerful Firebending blast that leveled the rock wall currently in front of me. Then the three of us raced forward.

Seeing this, the Avatar and his companions jumped onto his bison and flew off. The cowards didn't even bother to say good—bye.

We returned to our tank and continued to follow the trail of fur. It led to a clearing next to a river. Once again, we got out of the tank and surveyed the clearing on our mongoose—dragons.

I spotted a saddle and the remains of food supplies, signs that they had been here.

"The trail goes this way, Azula," Ty Lee announced.

Sure enough, a thick trail of white fur continued into the woods heading east. I looked at the river and noticed huge amounts of fur floating in the water. Then I glanced to the west and saw a wide swath of broken branches, leading in the opposite direction from the path of fur.

Why is there so much fur in the river? Of course! They must have finally realized that the beast is shedding, and that this is how we have been following them. They must have tried to wash off the creature's excess fur in the river so it would no longer leave an obvious path for us.

So then why is there a trail of fur leading away from the river to the east, when those broken branches show that the beast went the other way? Ah, someone must be using his brain, but he doesn't know who he's dealing with.

"The Avatar is trying to give us the slip," I told the girls.

Obviously, some of his group went in one direction, while others left some fur to give me the impression that they had gone the other way. I see that some of the fur along the eastern path is clinging to high branches. That means it was dropped from the air. If the beast went west, then the only one who could have flown east to drop the fur and mislead us was the Avatar himself—I had seen him fly on his glider back at Omashu.

This called for a change in plans.

"Ty Lee, Mai, you two head west, in the direction of those broken branches, and keep your eye out for the bison," I said. "I'm certain it went that way. I will follow this trail to the east, where I am sure I will find the Avatar!"

🀫 🀫 🀫

As my girls took off on their mongoose-dragons along the trail heading west, I rode mine heading east. How noble of the Avatar, willing to lead me away from the others to protect his friends, at the cost of his own freedom. And how foolish, too.

After following the trail for most of the day, I came to a deserted town. The sun was low in the sky and cast long shadows onto the abandoned buildings. There, in the center of the empty town, stood the Avatar, alone. I dismounted and walked toward him slowly.

He's smaller than he first appeared when he ran from me in Omashu. Brave Avatar, we shall soon see what you are made of.

"All right, you've caught up with me," he said boldly. "Now, who are you, and what do you want?" he asked.

I find it amusing that he tries to sound so tough, but he has the voice of a child! He has no idea who I am. I'll have to give him a little help. "You mean you haven't guessed? You don't see the family resemblance? Here's a hint."

I covered my left eye with one hand, then spoke in a low, raspy voice. "I must find the Avatar to restore my honor."

But there was no reaction. Boys can be so pigheaded about trying to maintain a tough exterior. "It's okay. You can laugh. It's funny," I said.

But he didn't laugh. He was no fun at all. Instead he asked seriously, "So now what?"

Fine. Be that way. I can play the serious warrior better than you. "Now it's over," I replied. "You're tired, and you have no place to go. You can run, but you know I'll catch you."

I didn't think he could look any more serious than he already did, but he narrowed his eyes and stared right at me. "I'm not running," he declared.

Very well. Let's just get to the point. "Do you really want to fight me?" I asked.

"Yes, I really do," replied a low, raspy voice from behind me.

"Zuko!" the Avatar cried, as shocked to see my brother as I was.

Well, well, well. A lovely little family reunion. Nice work, Zu-zu. I truly did not know that you have been following me. And I thought I'd have to track you down once I captured the Avatar. But now you have saved me the trouble. "I was wondering when you'd show up, Zu-zu."

The Avatar giggled. "Zu-zu?"

Of course this really annoyed my sensitive big brother. Zuko turned to me, his fists clenched, his eyes fierce.

"Back off, Azula," he said. "The Avatar is mine."

Oh, brother of mine, haven't you learned that I don't take orders from you—and I don't intend to start? "I'm not going anywhere, Zuko," I said.

The Avatar began sneaking away as though he thought he could take advantage of the conflict between Zuko and me. He is underestimating us. I immediately turned to face him and assumed a combat stance. Zuko did the same.

I can sense the Avatar's nervous energy. He's not sure who will attack him first or whether we will team up against him. Zuko is also fidgety. He's trying to hide it, but I know too well that he taps his leg nervously when he is worried. He has done this ever since we were kids.

I now have the unexpected opportunity to confront Zuko and the Avatar together. But who shall I deal with first? I have to make a choice.

I fired at Zuko, knocking him down. He returned a fireball as the Avatar tried to fly away. I dodged Zuko's strike while blasting the Avatar out of the air. He came instantly crashing back to the ground.

For a moment, Zuko and I teamed up against the Avatar, but I took advantage of our temporary alliance to once again attack Zuko. The strategic options presented in a three—way battle are quite intriguing. Still, I must remain alert to the movements of both of my opponents.

Zuko and I both hurled an enormous fire blast at the Avatar, but he flew into a nearby abandoned building, soaring up into the rafters. Zuko and I followed him into the building and discovered him floating on an air sphere. I shot a bolt of lightning at him, and as the sphere dissolved, the Avatar leaped to safety.

I will torch the entire town if I have to, but these two will not escape! I turned my attention back to Zuko for a moment. The force of my fire blast knocked Zuko out into the street. Then I turned back to the Avatar.

He ran into another building. I fired burst after burst of fire, which sliced pieces of the building away bit by bit. I now had the Avatar trapped.

I took a moment to savor the victory. The Avatar is mine. Nothing can change that! I sauntered into what was left of the building, and started a blaze that raced toward the Avatar. The look of terror on his face was priceless!

Seeking to prolong the moment, I drew back my hand slowly, preparing to unleash the final blow. Suddenly a thin stream of water slapped my hand down. Then the same water whip lifted the debris off the Avatar and released him!

Who dares to interfere with me?

"Katara!" the Avatar shouted.

I turned around in time to see a girl running from the building. Ah, she had been at Omashu with the Avatar. Well, this Waterbender will feel my wrath too!

I dashed after the girl, but the tall boy who travels with them also surprised me, attacking me with a boomerang. I stumbled backward.

But even working together, the Airbender, the Waterbender, and the boy with the boomerang posed little problem. I quickly regained my footing, then returned fierce fire of my own. That's when the ground began to shake violently, knocking me off my feet. This time I landed facedown in the dirt.

"I thought you guys could use a little help," said a voice from behind me. I scrambled to my feet and spun around.

The Earthbender! She has joined our little party. And she is not the only one. Iroh is here too! I knew that wherever Zu—zu was, Iroh would not be far behind.

"Uncle!" Zuko cried, sprawled on the ground.

"Get up," Iroh said, helping Zuko to his feet.

Let's see now, six against one. Over—whelming odds. I almost feel sorry for all of them. I feel as if my senses are heightened by this challenge. Attacks came from all directions — Earthbending, Airbending, Waterbending, and Firebending. I dodged them all, returning fire of my own with raging fury.

Then the group started closing in on me. Glancing over my shoulder, I saw that they were backing me toward a wall. Hmm . . . this will require just the right move at precisely the right time. But first I must distract them.

"Well, look at this," I said. "Enemies and traitors all working together. I'm done. I know when I'm beaten. You got me. A princess surrenders with honor."

I began to bow slightly, then quickly straightened up and blasted Iroh in the chest with my most powerful lightning strike. Down he went. Then the others reacted precisely as I knew they would.

The Airbender, Waterbender, Earthbender, my brother the Firebender, and even the boomerang boy all sent attacks flying toward me at the same moment. I easily danced out of the way, but the force of their combined blows sent up a huge explosion, blasting a hole in the wall behind me and filling the area with smoke and dust. It was the perfect cover for my escape!

I quietly slipped back to my mongoose-dragon and rode back toward the river. I wanted to find Ty Lee and Mai to plan our next move . . . but as it turned out, our next move came and found us.

50

降击神通

Chapter 4

The city of Ba Sing Se is the capital of the Earth Kingdom. It is where the Earth Kingdom ruler lives, and is the center of culture, education, finance, and agriculture as well.

My father and uncle knew that if Ba Sing Se fell, the Earth Kingdom would fall. If the Earth Kingdom falls, the Fire Nation will complete its destiny and control the entire world. Ba Sing Se is the key. Iroh tried years back to invade the walled fortress, but failed miserably. He didn't take the

Earthbenders' defenses and their resolve seriously enough, and it cost him dearly.

Since Iroh's failure, my father has been obsessed with taking Ba Sing Se. His war minister and generals have been working for years on a device to break through Ba Sing Se's fortified outer wall—an enormous drill. When I learned the drill was completed and on its way to the city, I knew that this would be the means to make up for my recent difficulties in capturing Iroh, Zuko, and the Avatar.

How sweet that I will be the one who finally completes the capture of Ba Sing Se. I will take command of the drill and lead the Fire Nation to victory. I will deliver the crushing blow that takes down the city and destroys the Earth Kingdom in one powerful assault. Once Ba Sing Se is in my hands, all else will become irrelevant. The Earth Kingdom will be ours, and the war will be over quickly— with my father in his rightful position as ruler of the entire world.

Mai, Ty Lee, and I caught up to the drill a short distance from Ba Sing Se. I immediately took command from the war minister, who had been leading the attack. He boasted that the drill would easily break through the outer wall of Ba Sing Se in a single day. Then he showed me the device.

The drill stood one hundred feet tall and was actually made up of two parts. The drill itself, which would bore an opening in the wall, was completely encased in a metal shell. The drill was connected to the shell by a series of braces, and the shell was impervious to any known substance or force.

I am thrilled! The drill is an incredibly efficient tool encased in armor that cannot be pierced. This machine is virtually unstoppable, and with it I shall begin the final phase of the Fire Nation's world victory!

I continued toward Ba Sing Se. The war minister remained with me and my crew, who ran the enormous contraption.

My father had also sent a fleet of small tanks to accompany the drill, in case we met any resistance. I laughed as I peered from the drill's command bridge at the tiny tanks, which looked like children's playthings flanking us on either side.

The view from the command bridge spread out before me as we approached the city. At my first glimpse of our target—the outer wall—the thrill of conflict swept through my bones. I live for conquest and success, and this time I will not fail my father.

"This drill is a feat of scientific ingenuity and raw destructive power," the war minister said as the wall drew closer.

He certainly does love his mechanical monstrosity. But his boasting grows tiresome. "Yes, so you've said," I responded.

"Once it tunnels through the wall, the troops accompanying us in the tanks will storm the city. The Earth Kingdom will finally fall, and you can claim Ba Sing Se in the name of your father. Nothing can stop us," the war minister continued.

Ty Lee leaned over my shoulder and peered out the window. "What about those guys down there?" she asked.

I followed her gaze and spotted a platoon of Earthbenders lining up in the path of the drill.

The war minister snorted his contempt for Ty Lee's concern. "Please. The drill's metal shell can handle any Earthbending attack."

He is really starting to get on my nerves. I need to cover all possibilities. I will take no chances. "Oh, I'm sure it can," I said. "But just to be on the safe side—Mai, Ty Lee, go take the Earthbenders out. I want nothing standing in our way."

"All right!" Mai cried as she and Ty Lee headed for the exit. "Finally something to do!"

I watched as the Earthbenders created a huge column of rock directly in our path on the battlefield below. The grinding tip of the drill pierced the rock tower, easily pulverizing it into dust, and the drill rolled steadily forward.

Well . . . perhaps the war minister is correct in his complete confidence in the machine. This may indeed prove to be an easy task. Father will be so impressed with me!

Ty Lee and Mai slid down the outside shell of the drill and leaped toward the

Earthbenders. Mai flung daggers to provide cover for Ty Lee, who bounced and tumbled her way to a large man—obviously the Earthbenders' captain. One by one, she struck key pressure points on his body, first blocking his bending ability, then causing him to collapse onto the ground. With their captain defeated, and Ty Lee and Mai gaining the upper hand, the Earthbenders quickly retreated. The girls slipped back inside the drill, which rumbled on, unimpeded, inching closer to the wall.

"This drill is so slow," Mai complained, falling back into the seat to catch her breath.

"Slow!" the war minister exclaimed. "Breaking through the outer wall of Ba Sing Se took General Iroh six hundred days!" he continued. "We will do so in one."

Mai shrugged. "Whatever."

Ty Lee suddenly pointed out the window at a cloud of dust rolling toward the drill. "Hey, look at that. It's so . . . poofy. You know. Poof."

What is that? Is there something hidden

within the cloud? I can't imagine it could be something that would pose a serious threat to this machine.

"Don't worry, Princess," the war minister said smugly. "I'm sure it's nothing. Just a harmless cloud of dust."

A few seconds later the cloud vanished, as if the drill had run right over it.

Maybe he was right. Perhaps it was simply a harmless dust cloud. Some trick of the wind. We continued forward, unhampered.

Suddenly the entire machine began to vibrate and hum. We shook and bounced for a few seconds, and then a high-pitched whirring sound cut through the dull din of the vehicle's motor.

We are in! The drill has hit the wall and begun its work, boring its way into the city. The assault on Ba Sing Se is under way at last!

"Congratulations, crew!" the war minister shouted into a metal pipe that served as the drill's communication system. "You can start the countdown to victory!"

However, a few minutes later the war minister's declaration proved to be premature. A bell rang, indicating an incoming message for the war minister on the communication system. In a panicked voice, a crew member informed us that an engineer had been ambushed, his plans for the drill had been stolen, and one of the braces that held the outer shell to the drill had been cut.

Sabotage! Somehow, someone has gotten into the drill and is trying to stop us from the inside! So that harmless cloud of dust was not quite so harmless after all. We must stop this threat before it spreads.

"Ladies, come with me!" I commanded, not even bothering to look at the war minister. I will deal with him after I finish handling this fiasco, for which I'm willing to bet my throne that the Avatar is responsible.

Ty Lee, Mai, and I hurried to the section of the machine between the drill and the outer shell. There, as I expected, we found the Avatar and his companions attempting to destroy another brace.

Very clever, Avatar. You may have snuck in here hidden by a dusty cloud, but you will never leave this drill alive! You have interfered with my plans for the last time.

I hurled a sizzling blast of blue fire at the Avatar, but he and two others dodged my attack. Then they split up. The Waterbending girl and the other boy ran one way, the Avatar in the opposite direction. I did not see the Earthbending girl with them.

"Follow them!" I shouted to Ty Lee and Mai. "The Avatar is mine!"

The Avatar disappeared around a bend. I followed up the chamber and emerged outside to find him Waterbending slashes into the metal armor at the top of the drill.

I unleashed a burst of flames at the Avatar, but he spun, and pushed my attack aside with his Airbending. He was also ready for my next attack, countering it with a huge gust of wind that swept toward me.

You are good, Avatar. But not good enough!

I launched myself over his airburst and landed beside him. Then I fired a swift series of short fire bursts one after another. But the Avatar slapped my hands aside with a whip made of water.

Impressive. His Waterbending skills have grown. But as everyone knows, fire evaporates water.

I focused my next blast right at his water whip. The whip sizzled into steam and vanished into the air. Just then, a flurry of rocks swept up from below, pelting both of us.

Earthbenders were attacking from the ground!

The Avatar redirected all the rocks at me, and I planted myself facedown on the surface of the shell to avoid them. After the rocks had passed me, I snapped back to my feet and blasted more fire at the Avatar. But he quickly formed more rocks into a wall, which deflected my flames. So he does have Earthbending skills as well now.

Thrusting each hand forward, the Avatar punched rocks at me. But I have come across attacks of this nature before. I drew myself up into the crane stance.

Balancing all my weight on one leg, I kicked the incoming rocks away with the shin guard on my raised leg, all the time moving closer to the Avatar and tossing fire at him.

Unable to counter my relentless onslaught, he moved backward, toward the drill.

There was nowhere for him to run! But I had no time to gloat. The Avatar suddenly drew loose rocks to him and formed a shield around his arm. He swung his rock gauntlet quickly and struck me in the stomach. Reeling backward, I spun around before regaining my footing. Just as I turned to charge at the Avatar, he was gone!

I looked all around the drill, but saw no sight of him. Then I looked up to see him running straight down the outer wall of the city. He could not be an easier target.

But as I drew back my hands, preparing to destroy him, the Avatar shocked me. He leaped from the wall, grasping a large pointed stone. He plunged downward, heading right for the slashes he had made in the top of the drill's armor.

I timed my blast perfectly. It struck the spot

where the Avatar landed—just as he drove the pointed rock into the shell. The armor tore open and the force of the Avatar's blow deflected my fire blast. Then a torrent of slurry, that sloppy mixture of pulverized rock and water that the drill funnels away as it digs deeper into the wall, slammed into me. Try as I might, I could not keep my footing on the slick metal surface, and the slurry knocked me from the drill.

No! I will not let the Avatar slip from my grasp again. Not when I'm so close!

And then it got even worse. I watched in horror as the entire drill vehicle collapsed, the braces having been split by the Avatar and his ragtag band. The weight of the outer shell buckled, then fell onto the drill mechanism itself, stopping the machine in its tracks. When I looked up, the Avatar had escaped again.

Then the back end of the drill opened and a gush of slurry poured out, depositing Mai and Ty Lee at my feet.

Mai looked up at me, stating the obvious: "We lost."

I was so angry I could barely respond. How much more time did I have to waste on the capture of the Avatar? It was clear that I needed to come up with another strategy.

Chapter 5

I need time to think, to plan. We failed at Ba Sing Se, and I have no intention of returning to the Fire Nation with news of another failure. My father gave me far more leeway than he ever gave Zuko, but he is not a patient man.

I left Ba Sing Se feeling a little depressed, but immediately felt better when, while traveling through the Earth Kingdom, we came upon more of the fur from the Avatar's beast.

Odd that the bison is so far from Ba Sing

Se—it must be separated from the Avatar. All at once I feel inspired. We will finally get the Avatar, and I will not have to waste any energy seeking him out: If I can capture his beast, the Avatar will come to me.

We followed the trail of bison fur into a thickly wooded area. It led us to a forest stream, where we eventually came upon three girls dressed in bright, colorful ceremonial costumes, standing in the stream bathing the Avatar's bison.

This search couldn't have been any easier! I fired a bolt of lightning to announce our arrival. It split a tree and startled the girls. The bison growled and snarled, but I could smell its fear. I waved a handful of its fur in the air. "My, my, you're easy to find," I said. "It's really astounding that my brother hasn't captured you yet."

The beast roared as the girls struck warrior poses—with fans! "Who are you, the Avatar's fan girls?" I asked.

"If you're looking for the Avatar, you're out of luck," one of them said.

"That's okay, any friend of the Avatar

is an enemy of mine," I replied as I fired a flaming blast at the girl, but the bison slammed the water with his tail, sending up a huge wave that extinguished the fire before it reached her.

While Mai and Ty Lee fought the other two girls, I launched a series of fiery attacks at the beast, and this time I could see fear in his eyes.

"Afraid of fire, I see. That's good, you should be," I said, before creating a ring of fire around him. Now the bison was truly terrified.

But one of the warriors doused the fire with mud from the stream. Now the animal had a way out.

"Go, Appa!" she shouted to the bison. "Get out of here! You have to find Aang. We'll be okay!" The beast took to the sky.

I turned my attention to this warrior, and knocked her off her feet with a leg sweep. I learned that these girls were warriors from Kyoshi Island—and quickly a plan took shape in my mind.

Ty Lee, Mai, and I returned to Ba Sing Se dressed as Kyoshi warriors. I was amazed at the warm reception we were given. The guards at the outer wall threw open the gates and welcomed us. An elaborately woven carpet was rolled out leading up to the palace. It was a little infuriating that Kyoshi warriors would garner such a welcome, but I will not complain just yet.

It's strange to think that all along I had only thought in terms of bigger and better weapons, of more complicated schemes to capture the Avatar. Yet all it takes is the right dress and makeup to open the door to the throne of the Earth Kingdom. And when all is said and done, that's exactly where I'll be seated.

The fancy carpet led directly to the king's throne. He stood as we approached. We paused before him and bowed respectfully.

"In our hour of need, it is with the highest honor that I welcome our esteemed allies, the Kyoshi warriors!" he announced to rousing cheers and applause from the gathered throng.

I bowed again and spoke softly. "We are

the Earth King's humble servants."

Following a formal welcoming ceremony, we joined the king in his throne room. There, he filled us in on the latest goings-on in Ba Sing Se. "It's been a difficult week. My most trusted adviser, Long Feng, and his Dai Li agents tried to take control of Ba Sing Se from me."

Tried? I believe we will have more luck than they did. "It's terrible when you can't trust the people who are closest to you," I said politely.

"But there is good news," added the king. "The Council of Generals is meeting to plan an invasion of the Fire Nation this summer—on the day of a solar eclipse, when Firebenders are at their weakest!"

Ah, that's their plan! All Firebenders dread the Day of Black Sun. It only comes every few years, but its effects are devastating. And while this news is shocking, I do not allow it to change my expression. Stupid Earthbenders; their plan will never come to pass—now that I am aware of their intentions.

The king has also foolishly told me all I need to know in order to successfully overthrow him. The key is the Dai Li. They are the elite members of an agency that keeps order in Ba Sing Se. I will gain control of them and set up a coup from within. And the delicious part is that the king won't even know who is taking over his throne!

Silly Earth King, you have handed the Fire Nation the ammunition it needs for its final victory. I must avoid eye contact with Mai and Ty Lee. They wear their emotions on their faces more overtly than I do. And I can't risk having the king suspect anything.

"Really? Now that sounds like a fascinating and brilliant plan," I replied with a smile.

We were led to the palace's most beautiful guest chambers, where I presented my plan to Mai and Ty Lee. "We have been given an extraordinary opportunity, girls. The chance to conquer Ba Sing Se."

I can see that I have shocked them. They are loyal companions and fine soldiers, but they lack any capacity for thinking beyond what is right before their faces.

"I thought we just wanted to capture the Avatar," Mai replied.

"Why settle for the Avatar when we can have the whole Earth Kingdom? For one hundred years we have tried to break into Ba Sing Se from the outside. But now we are here, inside, and we can take the city by ourselves."

Still they stare at me like wide-eyed deer. Looks like I will have to spell it out for them. "We have the king's trust, and so we are in a perfect position to organize a coup and overthrow him," I explained. "The key is the Dai Li. Whoever controls the Dai Li controls Ba Sing Se."

And I intend to control the Dai Li—without them even knowing it. First I have to get them to believe that they have the upper hand. I have spotted them spying on us as we moved about the city, although they are, of course, unaware that I know of their presence. A well-timed, well-rehearsed conversation for them to overhear our "plans" should plant the proper seed.

The following day I sent Mai and Ty Lee outside the palace while I waited just inside the doorway.

"How much longer do we have to serve the Earth King?" Mai asked.

"Princess Azula promised we would go back to the Fire Nation once we capture the Avatar."

"Shhh! Do you want the whole palace to know we're Fire Nation?"

I laughed to myself and was proud of the girls. The bait has been cast, and I'm certain the fish have bitten. Now to add a final convincing touch: I stepped into the palace with an angry look on my face, as if I'd just overheard their blunder. Mai and Ty Lee looked sufficiently ashamed. After a few minutes, when I was sure the Dai Li spies had scampered back into their holes to report this terribly interesting piece of news to their leaders, I dismissed Mai and Ty Lee. "Good work, girls," I said.

That night, still dressed as Kyoshi warriors, we returned to the king's throne room to continue the pretense of being his loyal servants. But the king was not there. And then another gift was handed to us.

The Waterbender who travels with the Avatar burst into the throne room. We retreated to the shadows, preparing for a fight, but the girl mistook us for real Kyoshi warriors, including one she obviously knew by name.

"Suki! It's Katara. Something terrible is going on," she cried. "The Fire Nation has infiltrated the city!"

How could word of our presence have traveled so fast that Katara is aware of it? And why would the Dai Li share information like that with her?

"I just saw Prince Zuko and his uncle!" she continued.

So THAT is what she means. I am relieved that she is unaware of our true identities, and very, very intrigued that Zu—zu is in the city. Things keep falling into place with each passing day. This scheme is indeed my masterstroke, destined to place me in Father's good graces forever.

"We have to tell the Earth King right away!" exclaimed Katara.

Oh, really? Well. I don't need to maintain this masquerade any longer. You are no match for the three of us, Waterbender. I stepped out from the shadows. "Oh, don't worry. I'll be sure to tell him."

Shocked, Katara pulled water from her pouch, but before she could bend it in an attack, Ty Lee was on her, blocking her chi. The water splashed harmlessly to the ground, then the girl crumpled into a heap at my feet. "Take her to the prison," I told the girls.

Katara will no longer trouble us, but I can't stop thinking about my brother. "I think it's time for a family reunion," I said as the girls left the room.

That night, before I had a chance to search for Zuko, several Dai Li agents slipped into my room and hurried me to the palace prison. I had been expecting something like this, and had instructed Mai and Ty Lee not to interfere. Now I must give the Dai Li the impression that I am outraged, and that I have no idea that they know exactly who I am.

The Dai Li brought me to Long Feng's cell. "What is this about?" I shouted, trying to sound as indignant as possible. "Your agents drag me down here in the middle of the night? You will not treat a Kyoshi warrior this way!"

"But you are not a Kyoshi warrior, are you, Princess Azula of the Fire Nation?" Long Feng replied with a smirk.

I flashed him my most convincing look of shock and dismay. "What do you want?" I asked.

I listened as he proposed a deal. He wanted to take back control of Ba Sing Se and he told me that I had something that he needed—the Earth King's trust.

"Why should I help you?" I asked. Come on, take the bait, step into my trap.

"Because I can get you the Avatar."

Perfect! He thinks he has me. "I'm listening."

I stood there and pretended to be interested in his plan to capture the Avatar and deliver him to the Fire Nation. I don't know if he's lying or not, but it really doesn't matter. Whatever he thinks he will do is incorrect: In the end he will do exactly as I want. So for now, I tell him that we have a deal. The look of satisfaction on the pathetic man's face is sickening.

As I head back to my chambers, I remind myself that it won't be long before Long Feng realizes how stupid he really is. All the wheels are in motion. Now we just have to put together the final pieces of my plan.

降击神通

Chapter 6

Even though I was nervous, I was not about to show it in front of the group of Dai Li agents I had gathered. Everything hinges on the performance I am about to give. I need their trust, but if I can't have that, I need to inspire fear. I have found that fear is a stronger motivator than trust, especially among those, like the Dai Li, who are used to operating along the shadowy edges of the rules.

"The Earth King and the Council of Generals do not trust the Dai Li," I said firmly.

"They imprisoned your leader, Long Feng. Next they will eliminate you. We must seize power at once. Our coup must be swift and decisive. The king and his generals must be taken out simultaneously. Then the military will fall under our control."

I have captured their attention. Now this is it, the moment in which I establish control. I really have to sell this.

"Long Feng has placed you in MY command while we overthrow the government. For some of you, it might be difficult and strange to ally yourself with a Fire Nation princess. But you must banish that prejudice from your heart."

I believe that if I make an example of one agent, the others will follow. Yes, this one looks suitably nervous. I'll stare at him directly in the eyes as I deliver the final piece.

"If I sense any disloyalty, any hesitation, any weakness at all . . . I will snuff it out!"

The agent bowed to me, refusing to stand back up until I had spoken. It couldn't have been more perfect. They are all now my servants. "That is all," I said dismissively.

The Dai Li hurried from the room, leaving only Ty Lee and Mai at my side.

"Nice speech, Azula!" Ty Lee said. "Pretty and poetic, but also scary, in a good way."

Precisely my intention. "I thought it went well," I replied. "But there are still a few loose ends—the Avatar, and my brother and uncle."

I sent a message to Iroh's tea shop—making it look as if the note had come from the Earth King—requesting that he and Zuko come to the palace as guests of the king, to personally serve him tea. There was no way Iroh could resist such an offer.

The next day, I watched from the shadows as Iroh and Zuko set up tea in the palace tea room.

I marveled at how soft and so pitifully domesticated they had both become. The once great general, who was called the Dragon of the West, and the Fire Lord's firstborn, preparing tea like servants. If my father could see his son . . . Well, no matter. Soon they will be back in the Fire Nation, or else they will be destroyed.

At a signal from me, the Dai Li agents entered the room.

"Something's not right," Zuko said, noticing their presence.

Smart boy. Something is most definitely not right . . . for you!

"It's teatime!" I announced as I stepped out of the shadows.

"Azula!" Zuko cried.

I could see the fear in his eyes. Still, he put on a brave face, stepping toward me as if he was ready to fight. A Dai Li agent quickly stepped into Zuko's path.

The loyalty of the Dai Li is without question. They are willing to lay down their lives to protect me. Excellent. This unwavering allegiance will be necessary in order to complete my ascent to the throne.

Iroh calmly sipped his tea. He is better at not showing panic than Zu–zu. "Did I ever tell you how I got the nickname Dragon of the West?" he asked.

I don't know which is worse: fighting Iroh, or being bored to death by one of his hopelessly longwinded stories. "I'm not interested in a lengthy anecdote, Uncle," I said impatiently.

"It's more of a demonstration, really," Iroh insisted.

Then he suddenly Firebended a blazing burst of flame from his mouth. The Dai Li scattered in all directions, and Iroh and Zuko ran from the tea room. The Dai Li and I chased them down the hall—and into a hallway that was a dead end. They were trapped!

But then Iroh did something that surprised me: He used a lightning attack to blast a hole in the wall and jumped several stories down to the ground.

"Come on, Zuko," he called from below.

"No," Zuko said firmly. "I'm tired of running. It's time I faced Azula."

"You're so dramatic, Brother," I said. "Are you challenging me?"

Zuko glowered. "Yes, I challenge you."

"No thanks," I replied, just as Zuko unleashed a powerful Firebending attack that was easily blocked by the Dai Li agents. They Earthbended a huge wall of rock to deflect the flames. Then the agents swarmed on Zuko, quickly subduing him.

Seeing this made me realize that as much as I enjoy a good fight, I could get used to having a squadron of agents handling my enemies for me every now and then!

The rest of my plan was quickly set in motion. With Katara and Zuko locked away in an underground prison chamber, I set the Dai Li to the task of arresting and imprisoning all the generals on the Council of Generals.

At long last, I will soon sit upon the throne of the Earth Kingdom.

🀙 🀙 🀙

We returned to the king's throne room, and this time he was there. Mai and Ty Lee took up their bodyguard positions on either side of the throne, and I once again lingered in the shadows.

A short while later, the other two members of the Avatar's party—the tall warrior boy and the Earthbending girl—rushed into the throne room. As the two approached the king, Ty Lee and Mai attacked. The Earthbender managed to put Mai on the defensive while the boy was able to avoid Ty Lee's chi-blocking moves.

Very skillful. But I have the upper hand in these matters. Now that the king knows that we are not really Kyoshi warriors, I can finally drop this annoying pretense. I stepped up to the king and placed my hand beside his head, preparing to strike him with a Firebending blow. I felt him stiffen with fear.

"This fight is over," I said.

The boy and the Earthbender stopped, seeing that the Earth King was in serious danger. "Get them out of my sight," I ordered. Mai, Ty Lee, and two Dai Li agents hauled everyone—including the Earth King—off to the prison.

I stood alone in the throne room—MY throne room, now that our little charade had ended. I'm going to like it here as ruler of the Earth Kingdom.

Then Long Feng walked in, surrounded by a throng of Dai Li agents. There was just one more step on my road to the throne: Long Feng was the final obstacle on my journey.

"It looks like the coup has gone perfectly," he said.

"It has," I responded.

"Now comes the part where I double-cross you, Azula. Dai Li, arrest the Fire Nation princess!"

Nobody moved. The Dai Li stood their ground. Ha! Long Feng, you are a fool. These men are smart enough to know that betraying me would have far more severe consequences than would turning their backs on you.

"They haven't made up their minds," I said, pleased with the agents' loyalty. "They're going to wait to see how this ends. To learn who will sit on the throne. They are not sure which one of us will bow down. But I know—and so do you, Long Feng."

I strode slowly to the throne and sat down as if I had always been in that seat. I stared at Long Feng, letting him think everything over. There is only one conclusion he can come to. Only one choice for him to make. And he knows it. He heaved a heavy sigh, then bowed to me.

"You've beaten me at my own game," he said heavily.

Don't flatter yourself, Long Feng. You were my pawn from the beginning. It's too bad that you've only now realized the extent of my power.

"You were never even a player," I said. Then I nodded to the Dai Li, who swooped down on Long Feng and took him to the prison.

Finally alone in my throne room, I took a moment to savor being ruler of the Earth Kingdom. Not bad for a fourteen-year-old.

But I still had to prepare myself to deal with Zuko.

I took a squad of Dai Li agents with me and headed for the prison chambers in the underground crystal catacombs. There, I overheard Iroh trying to convince Zuko to forsake his heritage, to turn his back on his destiny, and to oppose me.

When I reached their chamber, I immediately ordered the Dai Li to Earthbend a crystal cave around Iroh, so he couldn't help his nephew. Then I turned to face Zuko.

"I expected this kind of treachery from Uncle, but you, Prince Zuko, are no traitor. Are you? It's not too late, Zuko. You can still redeem yourself."

I know he doesn't believe Iroh and all his talk of turning to goodness. I know what Zuko wants deep in his heart. I have always known him better than anyone else. He can't hide his true feelings and desires from me, no matter what he says, no matter how noble a face he puts on for others. I know what choice he will make, even if he doesn't know.

Iroh had tried to persuade him not to join me, but I told Zuko that we needed to work as a team, to share in the conquest of Ba Sing Se, and to complete the Fire Nation's world domination together. What was more, I reminded him, was that he could restore his honor, capture the Avatar, and reclaim our father's love.

"You will have everything you want if you join me," I said patiently. "You are free to choose." Then I ordered the Dai Li to release him, sure of what his decision would be.

I must now turn my attention to the Avatar.

I caught up with him in the crystal courtyard—and he was with Katara! The Avatar must have released her from prison. I fired blasts of blue lightning that shot through the crystal walls, but Katara sent a sheet of ice beneath my feet. Then the Avatar Earthbended a rock ledge that knocked me down.

These two are proving to be worthwhile opponents.

We battled on until a huge red fireball suddenly exploded in the center of the courtyard. Zuko! For a split second I had a moment of doubt. Could I have been wrong, and he was attacking ME? It didn't take Zuko long to answer my question. He turned and released a barrage of fire—right at the Avatar.

My dear brother, you were born to be a prince of the Fire Nation, and now the time has come for you to fulfill that destiny by my side. Together we battled the Avatar and the Waterbender, who tried to make Zuko feel guilty about his choice. He hesitated for a moment, poor, weak Zu—zu, but then fired a blast at Katara.

She stumbled back into a stream. This is my chance! I fired a charge of lightning into the stream. It traveled through the water and struck Katara. She collapsed from the shock.

Then something unexpected happened. The Avatar's tattoos began to glow, and he seemed to grow in power—but he also appeared to be distracted by this strange state he had entered.

Now it ends, Avatar! I blasted him from behind with my most powerful lightning bolt. His tattoos stopped glowing and he crumpled to the ground. At the same time, Katara recovered. She quickly rushed to his side, but this fight was over.

Zuko and I approached the weakened girl and the motionless Avatar, and prepared for our final victory.

Suddenly a rush of fire and lightning filled the air, blocking our path to the helpless duo.

Iroh! The traitor has managed to free

himself. But he cannot take away my ultimate moment of glory. I will not allow it.

Although I defeated Iroh, he fought fiercely. By the time I was able to subdue him, Katara—and more important, the Avatar—had vanished.

And so the Avatar has escaped yet again. But unlike the other times, I am less upset about it, as I now have two great victories to celebrate.

I returned to the throne room and sat on my new throne, with Zuko standing beside me. "We've done it, Zuko. It's taken one hundred years, but thanks to us, the Fire Nation has conquered Ba Sing Se."

Zuko, however, was not in such a joyous mood. He falls back so easily into his moody, brooding habits. "I betrayed Uncle," he said, with shame in his voice.

"No, Brother, he betrayed you," I said. "When you return home, Father will welcome you as a war hero."

"But I don't have the Avatar. What if Father doesn't restore my honor?" he asked.

Poor, poor Zuko. I actually feel sorry for

him. He still doesn't understand, even at his moment of ultimate achievement.

"Father doesn't need to restore your honor, Zuko," I explained. "Today you restored your own honor."

My brother looked away from me with a pained expression across his face. I hope he can eventually believe what I have told him: that by choosing his family, by choosing me over the Avatar, he has come back to his rightful place in the Fire Nation.

And I welcome him by my side.

NICKELODEON

AVATAR
THE LAST AIRBENDER

THE EARTH KINGDOM CHRONICLES:
THE TALE OF
TOPH

by Michael Teitelbaum
based on original screenplays
written for *Avatar: The Last Airbender*

Simon Spotlight/Nickelodeon
New York   London   Toronto   Sydney

Chapter 1

My name is Toph Beifong. I'm an Earthbender. A pretty good one, too. But what really stinks is that I have to hide that part of who I am.

See, my parents are very rich and powerful. I come from one of the most important families in the Earth Kingdom, the Beifongs. Just saying my last name has always opened doors. People rush to help me just because my family is wealthy, and I really can't stand that.

I live on a huge estate in a giant mansion, with servants attending to my every whim. I hate that, too. I don't want to be treated as royalty or anyone special. And I most definitely do not want to be treated as if I have a handicap.

Oh, yeah, I guess I should mention that I'm blind. But before you start feeling sorry for me or start thinking I'm helpless, let me explain something. I see with my feet. I know it sounds weird, but believe me, it's true. More accurately, I see using Earthbending. I feel the vibrations in the earth and they help me figure out where everything is. I can sense the slightest movement—in other people, in tree branches swaying in the wind, even in the tiniest ants crawling on the ground.

I've never felt sorry for myself for one second, but my parents don't understand me. They always treat me like I'm helpless. They think I'm just a beginning-level Earthbending student, and they take comfort in that. If I ever showed them what I'm really capable of, they'd ground me for the next twenty years!

Sometimes I get so frustrated from hiding who I really am, not being able to use my Earthbending skills to their full capacity around my mom and dad, I feel like screaming! So, that's why I've adopted a kind of secret identity.

I sneak out of my house at night, when my

parents are asleep, and I compete in Earth-bending tournaments. If my folks ever found out about it, I'd be grounded for the rest of my life! At the competitions I'm known as "the Blind Bandit." It's kind of silly, I know. But I didn't even make up the name. This guy named Xin Fu, who runs the tournaments, started calling me that.

Competing lets me cut loose with my Earth-bending abilities—a chance I never get as Toph Beifong, poor, weak, blind girl, obedient daughter of the oh-so-important Beifong fam-ily. But as the Blind Bandit, I fight—and win, by the way. In fact, I'M the reigning champion!

Tonight is Earth Rumble Six. The arena is packed. After a particularly boring day "studying" with my Earthbending teacher, Master Yu, "learning" how to move tiny pebbles, I'm ready to kick some Earthbending butt.

As the champ, I get to sit back and watch a bunch of chumps compete until they narrow the challengers down. My opponent tonight is this big, muscle-bound guy who calls himself "the Boulder." I think he got the name because he moves as slowly and stomps as heavily as one, not because he Earthbends them well.

Okay, here it goes. . . . I love it when the crowd cheers like this!

"The Boulder feels conflicted about fighting a young, blind girl!" he said aloud.

What a fool! He's going down—hard!

"Whenever you're ready, 'Pebble'!" The crowd loves this stuff. And I have to admit I get a kick out of stirring them up.

Right now I'm laughing loudly. You know, to make the Boulder even madder than he already is. The angrier an opponent, the less subtle his attack, the easier it is for me to follow his moves and stop him.

"It's on!" the Boulder cried.

Finally! Okay, Toph, focus on his movements. Block out the sound of the crowd, just feel the ground under your feet. There he is—he's charging forward—but not for long!

The Boulder went down quickly. He took a big clumsy step toward me, then lifted his other foot. Before it could hit the ground, I flexed my ankle, driving my heel into the earth, sending a narrow shockwave racing toward him. So as his foot came down, a ripple of rock from my shockwave shoved his foot to the side, causing him to land in a painful split. He moaned and groaned as he scrambled back to his feet.

Ha! Take that! Maybe one of these days they'll bring me some serious competition. In fact, maybe I'll just finish him off right now—for kicks. BAM!

I extended my arms, Earthbending three jagged poles of rock, which burst up from the ground, slammed into the Boulder, and sent him flying into the far wall. Match over.

Yawn! This is so boring—Whoa, did I just hear that right? Xin Fu's offering a sack of gold to anyone who can beat me. Finally, some real competition. What, no takers? Wait a minute, who's this little guy? He feels tiny . . . small enough to crush with my bare hands—without even using Earthbending! What'd he just say to me? He doesn't want to fight, he just wants to talk to me? I'm not here for con-versation, kid. I'm here to defend my title, so bring it on!

Okay, he's in the air . . . but why hasn't he landed? Where'd he go? Is he still in the air? How can that be? I can't see him if I can't feel his movements on the ground. There he is. But he landed so softly, as if he was floating. How did he do that?

"Somebody's a little light on his feet!" I shouted. "What's your fighting name? 'The Fancy Dancer'?"

He's not getting away this time. I'll knock him right off those fancy feet.

He's gone, again! It's like he just vanished. Can this kid fly? That's impossible, but all I know is that he's not standing on the ground. Ah, there you are. An even softer landing this time. I am not amused.

Okay, no more funny business. You want to play, here's a ball, kid. Actually, here's a big fat boulder! Wait a minute, why can't I hear the boulder rolling toward him? What's happening?

BAM! I can't believe it! He just turned my boulder against me and it pushed me out of the ring! The rock never landed, and the Fancy Dancer never touched down. That must be why I couldn't pick up the rock's movement fast enough. And that's how this scrawny little kid beat me! I am so out of here!

"Wait!"

Now what? Oh, now he wants to chat!

"Please, listen!"

This kid just doesn't know when to quit!

"I need an Earthbending teacher, and I think it's supposed to be you!"

And this is my problem because . . . ?

"Whoever you are, just leave me alone!" Then I Earthbended a doorway through the wall, kept on walking, and slammed the opening shut behind me.

I don't know who this kid is or what he's talking about, but I really don't care. I'm no one's teacher, especially not some weird, flying dancer who just stole my championship title!

🪙 🪙 🪙

The very next day I was strolling the grounds of my family's estate when I felt three intruders scramble over the stone wall and land in the bushes. I guess they thought they were being quiet, but I can feel them through the earth, loud and clear. This'll surprise them.

WHOOSH! I made a mound of earth pop up beneath them, flinging them into the nearby bushes.

Surprise, surprise, the intruders are none

other than the Fancy Dancer and two of his friends! What does he want?

"What are you doing here, Twinkle Toes?"

"Well, a crazy king told me I had to find an Earthbender who listens to the earth. And then I had a vision in a magic swamp, and—"

What is this kid rambling on about?

The girl he was with interrupted him. "What Aang is trying to say is, he's the Avatar, and if he doesn't master Earthbending soon, he won't be able to defeat the Fire Lord."

The Avatar, huh? Well, that explains a lot! No wonder he was able to float through the air to evade me, and to redirect the boulder I shot at him. He can AIRBEND. So that's why Twinkle Toes is so light on his feet! Still, that has nothing to do with me.

"Not my problem. Now get out of here before I call the guards."

When they refused to leave I went into my helpless little girl act. I hate doing it, but some—times it serves its purpose. There's no way I'm going to let this guy ruin the cover I've got going. I cried out for the guards, who came running as they scrambled back over the wall.

"I thought I heard something," I told the guards. "I was scared."

"You know your father doesn't want you wandering the grounds without supervision!"

You know, it's funny that they think I'M the blind one. They're the ones who should open their eyes to the truth. Maybe someday I'll be able to be who I really am and not have to hide my ability. But not today.

🪙 🪙 🪙

Back at the house, my father pressed Master Yu about my Earthbending lessons. He wanted to make sure that I wasn't doing anything too dangerous.

"Absolutely not!" Master Yu said. "I'm keep—ing her at the beginner's level."

Ha! If he only knew! Of course, I had to sit there and listen to his nonsense, as usual. What kind of an Earthbending instructor can't spot potential and talent like mine? Like I said, I think they're the blind ones. I am so ready to break out of this . . . this prison.

Then one of the servants told my father that he had an unannounced visitor—the Avatar.

That kid just does not give up! Now he's wormed his way into my house using his title, which of course totally impresses my father. Well, I don't care what the Avatar does or says. I'm not going to become his Earthbending teacher. Besides, my father will never allow it.

So the Avatar and his two friends are joining me, my parents, and Master Yu for dinner. My parents are making such a fuss over the Avatar! I can tell this isn't going to be pretty. . . .

"Avatar Aang, it's an honor to have you visit us. You're welcome in our home as long as you like."

I think I'm going to be sick!

"In your opinion, how much longer do you think the war will last?" my father asked the Avatar.

"I'd like to defeat the Fire Lord by the end of summer, but I can't do that without finding an Earthbending teacher first."

I can feel him staring right at me!

"Master Yu is the finest teacher in the land," my father said. "He's been teaching Toph since she was little."

"Then she must be a great Earthbender!" the Avatar blurted out. "Good enough to teach someone else!"

What is he doing? This kid is going to get me into big trouble. He's going to blow every—thing. I can't let him tell my folks about my life as the Blind Bandit!

I slid my foot against the stone floor and sent an Earthbending jolt to the Avatar's leg. Hopefully that'll quiet him down.

"Sadly, because of her blindness, I don't think Toph will ever become a true master," my father said.

Just leave it at that, kid, all right!?

"Oh, I'm sure she's better than you think!"

Unbelievable! I expected the Avatar would be a little quicker on the uptake. Here, take another kick; maybe you'll get the message this time.

"What is your problem!" I shouted.

"What is YOUR problem?" the Avatar yelled, unleashing an Airbending blast that splattered soup all over everyone.

I wish he would just leave me ALONE!

I've spent most of tonight tossing and turning in my bed. Am I being too harsh? Am I taking out my own frustrating life on this kid who's just looking for some help? I should go talk to him.

When I walked into the Avatar's room, he jumped back and struck a defensive pose. I explained that I wasn't here to fight him and that I just wanted to talk. Isn't that what he said to me the first time we met? How ironic!

We took a walk through the estate's moonlit gardens, and I explained to him how I actually see through Earthbending. "But my parents don't understand. They've always treated me like I was helpless." He's kind of easy to talk to.

"Why stay here if you're not happy?"

He doesn't understand. They're my parents. "Where else am I supposed to go?"

"You could come with us."

He's got it pretty good, I suppose. He gets to go wherever he wants, without anyone telling him what to do. "You have a good life. It's just not MY life."

Just as I started to feel really sorry for myself, I felt movement nearby. People. Lots of them. All around us. "We're being ambushed. We've got to get out of here." I grabbed the Avatar's hand and hurried away, but a wall of earth rose up around us.

Earthbenders! Xin Fu and the others from Earth Rumble Six—I recognize their voices. How did they find me?

Before I could move, two metal cages dropped from above, trapping us inside.

I can't bend metal! Now there's no escape. Oh, no . . . they're hauling us away. . . . I think they are trying to get ransom money out of my parents!

✾ ✾ ✾

They brought us back to the Earthbending arena where a short while later my father and Master Yu showed up, along with the Avatar's two friends. The Avatar's friend named Sokka gave back the money the Avatar had won, and Xin Fu released me.

But I can feel that the Avatar is still locked in his cage. It seems that Xin Fu plans to turn him over to the Fire Nation. He and the other Earthbenders are starting to carry off Aang's cage.

I feel sorry for Aang, but what am I supposed to do? My father is right here. I can't give myself away; my life will be over. It's time for me to go. . . .

"Toph, there are too many of them," Katara, Aang's other friend (and Sokka's sister), called out to me. "We need an Earthbender. We need YOU."

"My daughter is blind, tiny, helpless, and fragile."

Even though I've pretended to be those things for so long, I'm not actually ANY of them, and hearing my father say that makes me so mad! You know what? I'm sick of pretending. Why should I have to hide who I am because my father can't accept me? If he loves me, he should love me no matter what. . . . Enough is enough. I can't let them take the Avatar away. Katara is right. If I don't help him, the Avatar will be handed over to the Fire Nation, and I can't let that happen.

"My daughter cannot help you," my father insisted.

"Yes, I can!" I let go of my father's hand and headed back into the arena.

18

"Let him go!" I shouted at the Earthbenders. "I beat you all before and I'll do it again!"

🈴 🈴 🈴

Fighting in front of my father felt amazing! The Earthbenders tossed Aang's cage aside and charged at me. One by one I slammed them with my Earthbending, blocking their attacks and hurling them out of the ring. For that one moment I wished wasn't blind—just so I could see the expressions on my father's and Master Yu's faces.

Then I battled against Xin Fu. It didn't take me long to beat him as well. Meanwhile Aang tricked one of the Earthbenders into smashing his cage, which freed him.

"Your daughter is the greatest Earthbender I've ever seen!" Master Yu said to my father.

I can only imagine what my father must look like.

🈴 🈴 🈴

Now that we've all calmed down a bit from what happened earlier, it's time to talk to my father and finally tell him the truth. Here it goes. . . .

"It's true. I've been sneaking out at night to

fight in Earthbending tournaments. I'm sorry I didn't tell you, but I didn't think you would understand. You've always treated me like I was helpless, but I'm not."

Maybe he'll understand? Maybe I'm not giving him enough credit and he'll finally give me the freedom I've always craved, now that he knows what I can do. . . . And maybe I'll finally get the chance to make friends, something I've never had because I've always been so sheltered (more like locked up).

"I've let you have far too much freedom, Toph. From now on you will be cared for and guarded twenty-four hours a day!"

Then again, maybe he won't. This is unbelievable! Too much freedom? Yeah right! I'm not allowed to do anything or go anywhere, how is that freedom? And now I can't even roam my prison by myself. . . . This can't get any worse. My life is over. I'm stuck here, truly a prisoner in my own home. Stuck being the powerless little girl I created.

And now he's telling Aang and the others to leave. He says they are no longer welcome in our house. Great. And I have to stand here and watch my first and only friend walk out the door and out of my life. . . .

🉐 🉐 🉐

I can't sleep—and the servant stationed at the edge of my bed isn't helping matters any. My mind is racing, but all I can think of is spending the rest of my life stuck here in this room in this house, burying who I really am deeper and deeper until she disappears completely.

Then Aang's words came drifting back to me. "You could come with us."

Aang is right. I DO crave the freedom that he and the others have. I DO want to experience the world, travel, and mostly stop pretending that I'm someone I'm not. I'm special. I can do things no one else can do. And if my father refuses to see that, then that's his problem. I'm twelve years old—old enough to know what I want—and I want to go with Aang. I want to teach him Earthbending. I want to have friends.

But how do I get away from this watchdog at the end of my bed, who follows my every move? Well, let's try this and see what happens. . . .

"I'm just going to the bathroom. I'm a big

girl. You don't have to come with me." That was easy! I tiptoed out of the room and locked the bathroom door. Silently, I slipped out the bathroom window. When I reached the ground I dashed through the gardens and leaped over the wall to freedom.

I only hope I'm not too late! I hope they haven't left yet! YES! There they are, at the top of the hill. But wait, I can't tell them the truth. I can't let them know that I disobeyed my father and ran away. I don't want them to tell me what I did was wrong, and I don't want Aang to feel responsible for my decision. This is my choice. Mine alone.

"My dad changed his mind," I lied. "He said I'm free to travel."

"You're going to be a great teacher, Toph," Aang said.

Wow, they're really excited that I can come. No one's ever really seemed to want me around or to miss me when I'm gone. It's kind of a nice feeling.

So, here I am, flying on the back of Aang's bison, with the whole world stretched out before me. Freedom! At long last, freedom!

Chapter 2

After flying for many hours we finally landed to set up camp for the night. I slid down off of Appa's back, and my feet touched nice, soft grass. At least it felt like grass. Turns out it was fur—bison fur. It's spring and Appa has started shedding something fierce.

I gathered up some fruit, nuts, and berries, so I'm all set as far as food goes. I'm just settling down against a rock and stretching out, drinking in my first full day of freedom— Ah, this is the life! Oh, here comes Katara. Wonder what she wants?

"So, Toph, usually when setting up camp,

we try to divide up the work between us."

"Hey, don't worry about me. I'm good."

Apparently she doesn't get it. She's going on and on about fetching water, building a fire, putting up the tents—all this stuff that has nothing to do with me. I can take care of myself. I always have. I don't need to be treated like a little kid. This is why I left home!

I get it—Katara is all rah-rah, go team. But the whole team thing just isn't my style. I've always been a loner, and just because I'm traveling with these guys doesn't mean I'm part of some group or something. I do stuff for ME. I carry my weight, without asking for anybody's assistance, like some dependant child. And they should do the same!

"I don't need a fire, I already collected my own food, and look . . ."

A quick Earthbending move should take care of a tent for me. A nice tent with rock walls. There! All done. "My tent's all set up!" But still Katara still doesn't look satisfied.

"Well, that's great for YOU. But we still need to finish—"

She really is annoying. What does she

want from me? I'm risking everything to come with them to help Aang learn Earthbending, and she won't stop hounding me about tents and water and firewood? I didn't leave home after being bossed around my whole life by my parents to be bossed around by her! "I don't understand what the problem is here!"

"Never mind . . ."

⊕ ⊕ ⊕

Later she came and apologized, saying that she was tired. Maybe that's why she's so cranky. I guess I should try to give her the benefit of the doubt. I accepted her apology and slipped into my rock tent to settle down for the night.

I had just fallen asleep when powerful vibra—tions rumbling through the earth woke me up. What is that? If I put my palms flat onto the ground, I'll be able to feel it.

This is something big. Very big. Whatever it is, it's powerful and it's heading our way.

I woke the others and suggested getting out of here. We scrambled onto Appa and took to the sky. Looking down they spotted a huge tank with thick treads and big missiles racing toward the spot where we had set up camp. We've got to get away from it, whatever it is.

We landed a good distance away. I stood for a moment and focused but felt no rumbling at all from that thing. We decided to settle there for the night, and that's when Katara started in again, asking me to help unload everybody else's stuff. I told her that I didn't ask her help unloading my stuff. How many times do I have to tell her that I carry my own weight!

"Ever since you joined us you've been selfish and unhelpful!" Katara screamed suddenly.

Selfish! I can't believe she said that. Selfish? I leave my cushy life to come here to help them and she thinks I'M selfish? I don't know what kind of fairy-tale world she's living in. "Listen, Sugar Queen. I gave up everything I had so I could teach Earthbending to Aang. So don't talk to me about selfish!"

I am done talking to the little princess. All I need is an earth tent—There! Now I'm shutting you out. In your face, sweetheart! I'm getting some sleep. Whoa—it's that thing again! I can feel it barreling toward us! Time to move, again!

For our third resting place we flew up to the top of a mountain. We all thought we'd be safe here, that the tank thing couldn't possibly find us much less follow us here. But we were wrong. I felt the vibrations shortly after we stopped. Then the others caught sight of black smoke rising over a hill, and now that thing is actually climbing up the mountain!

How does it keep finding us? Who's driving it? And what do they want with us? Katara and Sokka said they think it might be this guy named Zuko, the Fire Nation prince, who's been following them all over the world. Aang thinks we should stay and face whoever it is.

The tank just opened up! Three girls riding on mongoose—dragons are galloping toward us. Katara said she recognizes them as three girls they had fought in Omashu, before they picked me up.

Maybe Aang's right. Maybe we should just stand our ground. Between my bending, Aang's bending, and Katara's bending we should be able to take them. And if that doesn't work, Katara could always nag them to death.

☯ ☯ ☯

Well, we're off on Appa, again. I had raised a wall of rock to block the girls, but one of them Firebended right through it! So we decided to leave again. But, as Aang pointed out, we can't keep flying forever. I, for one, am so tired I can't even think straight. And neither can Appa, apparently, because he just started to fall asleep in midair! I hate flying. Now we really have to land!

"Okay," Sokka said as we landed. "We've put a lot of distance between us and them. The plan right now is to follow Appa's lead and get some sleep!"

"Of course, we could've gotten some sleep earlier if Toph didn't have such issues with helping," Katara blurted out.

I can't believe she's still going on about that. I never asked any of them for anything. I've carried my weight from the start. Is she just trying to make me the scapegoat? That is so unfair. Besides, if this is anyone's fault, it's that big flying fur ball!

"If there's anyone to blame, it's Sheddy over there!" I just can't help myself anymore. If they want to play rough, I'll play rough!

"You're blaming Appa!"

Okay, Aang's mad.

"He's leaving a trail of fur everywhere he goes! That's how those girls have been follow—ing us."

"How dare you blame Appa! He saved your life three times today. If there's anyone to blame, it's you. You're always talking about how you carry your own weight. But you're not carrying your weight. Appa is. And he never had a problem flying when it was just the three of us and Momo!" (Momo is their pet lemur.)

I really hate it when people yell at me. If I wanted to be bossed around and yelled at, I could have just stayed home. Besides, what I'm saying is true! I might be blind, but I'm obviously the only one who can see that's how these girls have been following us. This is why I risked my relationship with my parents? This is who I'm traveling around like a nomad for? This is the kid who tracked me down and snuck into my house and hounded me to be his teacher? And now suddenly I'm nothing but deadweight to him and a punching bag to his friends? I don't need this. I don't need any of this!

"I'm out of here." I don't know where I'm going, but anyplace has got to be better than this.

⊕ ⊕ ⊕

I can't stop thinking about what happened earlier. All my life I've wanted to leave home, to be free, to travel and experience things and do whatever I wanted. This trip is supposed to be my chance. I've even gotten used to the idea of teaching the Avatar—it would have been kind of cool. But I never expected to be treated that way.

Katara wants me to behave the way she thinks is right. I had enough of that at home. And Aang—I never thought he would turn on me like that. I can't believe I was actually starting to trust him. I won't make that mistake again. With anyone. Besides, I—

Wait a minute—there's someone over there, I can feel him moving. A quick Earthbending shove should surprise him.

WHOOSH! I slammed my heel into the ground, sending a ripple that passed under the rock and struck the man hiding there—a heavyset man from the way he hit the ground.

I'm back on the rock, ready for my next attack, but he's just lying there, moaning.

"Ouch, that really hurt my tailbone."

Turns out he's just an old man. Nothing to worry about.

Then he did the weirdest thing: he invited me to his campsite for a cup of tea. Sure, why not. I've got nothing else to do, nowhere I HAVE to be.

"You seem a little too young to be traveling alone," he said when we reached his campsite.

"You seem a little too old."

He laughed. Then he poured a cup of tea and handed it to me. He wouldn't even let me pour my own tea. He's just like everyone else. "People see me and think I'm weak. They want to take care of me. But I can take care of myself."

"You sound like my nephew! Always think-ing you need to do things on your own, without anyone's support. There's nothing wrong with letting people who love you help you. Not that I love you—I just met you."

He may be a little cuckoo, but maybe he knows what he's talking about. It's just so hard to trust people. How do I know someone I trust won't turn on me, like Aang did? How do I protect myself from getting hurt? I guess I can't; not fully anyway. But maybe that's okay. Maybe that's just the chance I have to take if I'm going to have friends. Hmm, this old guy might be on to something. . . .

"So . . . where's your nephew?"

"His life has recently changed, and he's going through very difficult times, so he went away and I'm tracking him. He doesn't want me around right now, but if he needs me, I'll be there."

It's kind of amazing how much this old guy cares about his nephew. I mean, even though he ran away, this guy still understands that his nephew needs to figure it out on his own. I wish my parents understood that. . . . Anyway, I guess in order to care that much about some-one, you HAVE to trust them; and in order to do that, you have to actually let them inside. So you might get hurt, big deal! I can handle that. . . . After all, I am the Blind Bandit!

"Your nephew is very lucky, even if he doesn't know it." Okay, Toph, time to get out of here and go find Aang. "Thank you."

"My pleasure! Sharing tea with a fascinating stranger is one of life's true delights."

"No . . . thank you for what you said. It helped me."

Come to think of it, I was pretty harsh to Aang. He was only looking out for Appa, and it did sound like I was attacking Appa when I said the thing about him shedding. And I was kind of hard on Katara too. She's right; I have to learn to be part of the team now. Needing them isn't so bad. It's not like I LOVE being on my own. I've just been alone my whole life, because no one ever knew the real me. But Aang, Sokka, and Katara like me for who I really am, and for the first time in my life I can have friends. For the first time, I don't have to be alone. I've got to find them. Whatever happens next, I'm better off with them than without them.

"Maybe you should tell your nephew that you need him, too."

I left the old man, and now I'm heading back toward where I left everyone—but wait—I'm picking up the vibrations of a tremendous battle being fought. This fight is major! Powerful bending energy is being released, even buildings are crumbling! I have to follow these vibrations. . . .

What is this place? An abandoned city? There's Aang, Katara, and Sokka. They're battling that powerful Firebender who was following us in the tank. And there's that guy Zuko that Aang was telling me about, and— the old guy I just met? Something strange is going on here. . . .

Okay. Turns out the Firebender is Princess Azula of the Fire Nation. And to my surprise, the old man I met in the woods is actu- ally Zuko and Azula's uncle Iroh; he's fighting Azula. I can't believe that cool, old guy is from the Fire Nation, and I can't believe he's related to the Fire Lord. . . . But I can't think about that now. . . . Now it's time to get in on the action and blast Princess Azula's tights off.

WHOOSH! I cut loose an Earthbending blast, knocking Azula off her feet. "I thought you guys could use a little help," I called out to Aang and the others.

"Thanks," said Katara. Even SHE'S glad to see me. Time to corner the princess and see how tough she is, then. . . .

She seems to be accepting her defeat. . . . But wait! Oh, no! She just blasted my new friend, her uncle, down to the ground. I hope he's all right! He was so kind to me. Azula's going to pay for this!

We all simultaneously unleashed powerful bending blasts at her, but it's too late. She's gone, and Zuko's tending to his uncle.

"Zuko, I can help," Katara offered.

"Leave!" he shouted back, unleashing a fire blast just above our heads.

So we're back on Appa, flying away. I'm glad to be back with my friends. It feels like the right place to be, the place where I belong now. I'm ready to start teaching Earthbending to Aang. But right now, I'm just happy to finally get some sleep.

Chapter 3

We're camped in a rock quarry, which is turning out to be the perfect location to begin Aang's training. After a good night's sleep last night, I woke up early this morning—but not as early as Aang—who was already wide awake and raring to go hours before me.

"So, what move are you going to teach me first?" he asked anxiously. "Rock-a-lanche? The Trembler? Ooh, maybe I could learn to make a whirlpool out of land?"

"Let's start with Move-a-Rock."

This kid has no clue how hard this is. Time to see what he makes of these two boulders.

"The key to Earthbending is your stance. You've got to be steady and strong. Rock is a stubborn element—if you're going to move it, you've got to be like a rock yourself."

A little demonstration: just a quick thrust of the arms and WHAM! Right into the wall!

"Okay, you ready to give it a try?"

"I'm ready," he said without hesitation.

Okay, his feet feel set, and he's mimicking my movement. That's good. Ready, set, and—WHAT!? Great, instead of the rock moving, Aang just flew backward across the quarry. He's not firm, not thinking like an Earthbender.

"Maybe if I came at it from another angle—"

"No! You've got to stop thinking like an Airbender. There's no clever trick, no different angle to approach the problem. You've got to face it head on! Be rocklike. I see we've got a lot of work to do, Twinkle Toes!"

This is not good. He's still fancy dancing, tiptoeing his way around the rock. He'll never move it that way. Being light on his feet may be great for Airbending, but it's never going to help him become an Earthbender. Feels like

Katara is coming over to tell me something. I wonder what she wants. . . .

"Toph, I've been training Aang for a while now. He responds to a positive teaching experience—lots of encouragement and praise."

Here she goes, bossing me around again. And this time it's about something I know and she doesn't—Earthbending! I don't want to start arguing again, but how could treating him like a baby and encouraging his whining possibly help his Earthbending at all?

"Thanks, Katara. I'll try that."

Whatever, I'm just going to humor her. That is, until she's gone. Then I'm going to ride Aang hard until he learns what he needs to know.

For Aang's next series of exercises, I set up an obstacle course. I had him lift heavy boulders and move them through the course. Then I covered myself in rock armor and told him to try to stop me from pushing him. With Aang balanced on two rock pillars, I had him bend some smaller rocks from hand to hand. Then I suddenly slammed a section out of each of the pillars to see if he could balance . . . and he hasn't fallen, which means he's actually holding his stance! Finally he's taking a step forward.

Okay, now it's time for a more challenging test. Instead of moving a rock, I think I'll
make him try to stop a rock. Yeah, stop it or be
crushed by it. Simple but effective motivation.

"Okay, Aang, I'm going to roll that boulder down at you. If you have the attitude of an
Earthbender, you'll stop the rock."

Just then Katara butt in again. "Sorry,
Toph, but are you sure this is best way to teach
Earthbending to Aang?"

Hmm, I have an idea. Sorry, Aang, but your
good friend just made things a little harder for
you. She's gonna love this. . . . "I'm glad you
said something, Katara. Actually there is a
better way." Better, not easier.

I put a blindfold on Aang. Now he'll have
to feel the vibrations of the boulder to stop it.
Welcome to my world! "Thank you, Katara."

"Yeah," Aang said, obviously unhappy with
Little Miss Buttinski. "Thanks, Katara."

Okay, the boulder is on its journey down the
hill, and Aang is getting into his horse stance.
Good. His form feels perfect, his stance feels
good. Now it's time to see whether or not he

has the courage to stand his ground. Here we go. . . . That's good, just keep sticking your ground, be rocklike and sense the vibration. Come on Aang, you can do this. . . . It's getting closer, I can feel it, it's time to—What happened? Either it flattened him or he pulled a fancy-dancer move and jumped out of the way. . . . Well, he didn't get flattened because I can feel him coming toward me.

"I guess I just panicked . . . I don't know what to say."

"There's nothing TO say. You blew it. You had perfect stance and perfect form." What am I going to do with him? How can I teach him Earthbending if he's scared to Earthbend? How can the Avatar, who's supposed to save everyone, be such a wimp? "When it came right down to it you didn't have the guts. Do you have what it takes to face that rock like an Earthbender?"

"No. I don't think I do."

Great. Now I'm supposed to feel bad about hurting his feelings? HE messed up, and HE should feel bad about that. I'm not Katara, I'm not going to console him and let him cry on my shoulder. But here comes the Sugar Queen to make it all better.

No wonder he can't learn anything. He's so used to being treated like a little baby by Katara that he doesn't know what it's like to not always get everything right the first time around. The minute things get hard he gives up, and she rewards him for it. She thinks working on Waterbending is going to make him feel better. Well, it might do that, but it won't make him any better at Earthbending. I can't teach him if he doesn't have the courage to stand up to that rock.

Hmm. That gives me an idea. Maybe if I can get him to stand up to me, standing up to the rock won't seem so tough. Maybe if I get him mad enough . . . this ought to bug him.

"Hey, Aang, I found these nuts in your bag. I figured you wouldn't mind, and if you did, you're too much of a pushover to say anything."

He doesn't mind? He's happy to share? Blah, blah, blah, all this nicey—nice Avatar stuff is starting to get to me. Well, this next part will definitely bug him.

"I also have this great new nutcracker."

I dropped a nut onto the ground and smashed it open with his staff.

I felt him wince. He's getting testy now.

"Actually, Toph, I'd prefer if you didn't. That's an antique handcrafted by the monks."

Is this kid for real? Get angry, will you! I've just gone through your stuff without asking, and now I'm basically destroying your staff, and all you can say is "you'd rather I didn't"?

Here comes Katara again. What now?

"Aang, it's almost sundown and Sokka isn't back yet."

The two of them are heading off to find Sokka. I'll trail behind, just in case.

A short while later Aang found Sokka. Looks like he's wedged into a crack in the ground, playing with a little moose–lion cub. Where there's a cub, there's a mom . . . and there she is; I can feel her, not to mention smell her. Boy, she's huge, and she's NOT interested in playing. I could easily Earthbend Sokka out, but this will be a good test of Aang's courage. I'll just stay here, behind the tree, and listen. If things get out of hand, I'll step in.

No, no, no, no. Aang's using Airbending to push the lioness away. What is wrong with this kid? I thought he wanted to be an Earthbender. Doesn't he realize his fancy dancing isn't keeping her away? She'll do anything for her cub, and tiptoeing and floating around isn't going to stop her. Okay, wait a minute. I think he's getting ready to try some Earthbending. He's preparing an Earthbending stance; I can feel his feet firmly planted in the ground. Here we go. He's going to Earthbend . . . and . . . silence. What just happened? He didn't Earthbend, and yet I can feel the lioness moving backward, away from him. She's taking her cub . . . and she's leaving.

That's it, Aang! You stood your ground and it worked! That's what it's all about. This deserves a round of applause.

"You were here the whole time?" Aang asked when he heard me clap. "Why didn't you do something? Sokka was in trouble—I was in trouble!"

"Guess it just didn't occur to me." Okay, I'm just going to remind him that I still have his staff, and he should be good and angry . . . and ready for my final test.

I dropped a nut on the ground and lifted Aang's staff, preparing to slam it down.

"Enough. I want my staff back."

Perfect! He's furious with me. Exactly what I hoped for. "Do it now! Earthbend, Twinkle Toes! You just stood your ground against a crazed beast, and more impressive, you stood your ground against me. Do it!"

Okay, here we go, for real this time. He's setting himself up in a rock-solid Earthbending stance. Good positioning. Good form. Now, just thrust your arms forward, stay steady, and move that rock!

WHOOSH! Bingo! This time I definitely felt something move. "You did it, Aang! You're an Earthbender!"

And I'm a pretty good teacher—way better than Master Yu, anyhow.

"This is really touching, but can someone get me out of here?" Sokka blurted out.

"No problem," Aang said, preparing to Earthbend Sokka free.

"I'll do it, Aang. You're still new at this—you might accidentally crush him."

"Yeah, no crushing, please!"

Chapter 4

I've been working really hard with Aang every 45 day for the past few weeks. He's improved his Earthbending and Waterbending significantly. We're all pretty tired from training and travel— ing, so we've decided to take short vacations.

At first Sokka objected, saying that we needed to find a map of the Fire Nation and come up with a plan to stop the Fire Lord once Aang was ready. But we promised him we'd spend his vacation tracking down the Fire Nation intelligence he was so keen on get— ting and he quieted down. He might be a total goof sometimes, but I do kind of admire his determination to kick some Fire Nation butt. Anyway, it was Katara's turn first, and she chose to go to the Misty Palms Oasis. Peace and quiet, here I come!

☯ ☯ ☯

We arrived at the place only to find that it was a rundown cantina—so much for lounging by the lake. But we did meet Professor Zei, head of anthropology at the university in Ba Sing Se, the Earth Kingdom's capitol. He told us he was searching for a library built by a great knowledge spirit named Wan Shi Tong. The library was hidden somewhere in the desert and was supposed to contain knowledge from all around the world.

Sokka got all excited because he decided that we're going to spend his vacation in the desert searching for the ancient library. He thinks that the library will have maps and other information about the Fire Nation.

If you ask me, that sounds like a horrible vacation. Who cares about some old library? I mean, I get that he's after the Fire Nation and all, but I really hate the desert. I just can't feel anything out there in the sand. I know there are some Earthbenders that live in the desert. They're actually called Sandbenders. In fact, there were quite a few hanging around the cantina when we arrived. But I can't Sand-bend, which basically means that in the desert I'm blind—really blind—without Earthbending to help me see. I'm not looking forward to this trip, but what can I do? I'm part of this team now, and there's no turning back. So, here we go, up onto Appa and off to the desert.

This is so boring! I can't even see, and I know there's absolutely nothing out there. Then the professor tells us that this place may not even exist! Great. This is most definitely not my idea of what a vacation should be. I've had enough of this. Time to have a little a fun.

"There it is!" Ha! Made them look. I can't believe they all listened to me! People, I'm blind, remember? "That's what it'll sound like when one of YOU spots it."

"Wait, down there," Sokka said anxiously. "What's that?"

Finally! Thank goodness! Time to land and get this over with already.

"Forget it," Katara cried suddenly. "It's obviously not what we're looking for. The building in this drawing is enormous."

"What kind of animal is that?" Sokka asked.

"That could be one of Wan Shi Tong's knowledge seekers, taking the form of a fox!" the professor said excitedly. "We must be close to the library!"

"No, this IS the library," Sokka said. "It's completely buried in the sand."

"Buried?" the professor cried as we landed. Then he fell to his knees. Is he going to start weeping? He must think the library is ruined. Okay, Toph, time for a little reconnaissance, feel things out and see what the story is.

This stone spire is definitely part of a huge building, and it feels like that building is buried beneath the sand. But it feels whole.

"Guys, the inside seems to be completely intact . . . and it's huge!" This library must hold every book and map ever made.

Apparently the knowledge seeker they were talking about climbed through a window on the side of the building. The others decided to follow it. Not me. Books don't do much for me. So I'm waiting outside with Appa.

Geez, Appa sure does scratch himself a lot. Talk about boring. When are they going to come back? I hope they find their maps and books and whatever else they wanted to get out of the library, or else this is a huge waste of time—Whoa, what's going on? I can't feel anything! Everything is shaking and the sand beneath my feet is disappearing. . . . Is the library sinking? If I could just get over there and feel it, I'd be able to tell—Oh no, it IS sinking. And everyone is still inside! This is awful. I've got to stop it. I have to keep the library from disappearing or the others are doomed. Who knows how far down it will sink?

This is why I hate sand—you can't get secure footing in grains that keep moving. I'm going to have to go ahead and do it anyway. Okay, fists tight, feet rooted . . . now push hard. Come on Toph, keep it from sinking! Fight the gravity, fight back!

What am I thinking? I can't hold this build-ing up forever. I'm not THAT strong. My feet keep slipping in this stupid sand. Come on, guys, get out of there—NOW! Please, hurry!

What's that rumbling? It sounds like it's coming from far away? Is something coming toward me? I can't deal with a new threat; I can barely handle this one! Well, whatever it is, it's moving very, very quickly. "Who's there?"

The sand, it feels like it's moving, and I'm not doing it. It's swirling around and around. That can only mean one thing: Sandbenders. What could they want?

Oh, no. They want Appa! How can I help him without letting go of the library and losing my friends inside?

I can hear the Sandbenders throwing ropes on Appa from every direction. They're trying to capture him. I can't just stand here! I have to let go and throw some earth their way, to slow them down. . . . WHOOSH! Take tha— Great. A sloppy cloud is all I can muster up? On solid ground I would have blasted them away. I'm useless here . . . and the library's sinking faster now than before!

What do I do? Let the library sink and try to stop the Sandbenders from taking Appa, or stop the building from slipping and lose Appa?

I can't win! I just can't. I'm sorry, Appa. I don't think I can help you in all this sand, but at least I have a small chance of saving Aang and the others. You understand that, don't you? Don't you? I'm sorry, buddy.

If the library would just stop sinking! I can't hold it! Where are you Aang?

Oh, wait, I can hear something. I hear people talking. They're out. Phew! I can finally let this thing go. Whoa, it's sinking all the way down, it's so far down I can't even feel it. . . .

Okay, now comes the hard part. Harder even than holding up that building. How do I tell Aang that I let those Sandbenders take Appa? That I couldn't stop them? I don't know how to tell him. I don't know what to say. I don't know how to make it better. I failed and I can't remember when I ever felt this bad.

"Where's Appa?" Aang asked.

I don't know, Aang, I don't know. . . . Be strong, Toph, and just tell him the truth.

"How could you let them take Appa?" Aang shouted. "Why didn't you stop them?"

"I couldn't stop them. The library was sink-ing. You guys were inside." Nothing he can say could make me feel any worse than I already do. And no explanation I give will be good enough. His best friend was taken. I'd be mad too.

"You could have come to get us! I could have saved him!"

"I can hardly feel vibrations out here. They snuck up on me. I couldn't do both—"

"You just didn't care! You never liked Appa! You wanted him gone!"

First the shedding comment and now this! No wonder he thinks I don't care about Appa. But that's not true, I promise! I never wanted this to happen. If we were on solid ground, I would have taken those guys apart. But I can't fight in the sand. I just can't. He's so mad at me . . . my first real friend, and this happens.

"Aang, stop it," Katara said. "You know Toph did all she could. She saved our lives!"

I guess I can't complain about Katara anymore; she's going to bat for me. Not that it matters, Aang isn't listening to her. Wow, he must really hate me if he won't even listen to Katara. And now he's flying off to try to find Appa. We're going to start trudging across the desert. I hope we spot Appa. . . .

Walking through the desert is so hard! I keep bumping into Sokka because I can't really feel where I'm going. And Katara has to keep turning me in the right direction so I don't wander off. Without a doubt, this is the low point of my entire life. Aang hates me, and I'm probably going to be stranded in the middle of the desert forever, and for the first time in my life, I actually FEEL like a blind girl. As we walked, Katara told me that in the library they discovered that there's going to be a solar eclipse soon and that if we get the Earth King to attack the Fire Nation on that day, the Fire Nation will be powerless without sun. If we get the Earth King to agree to the plan, we could actually defeat the Fire Nation. Imagine that?

After a long time Aang finally returned, having seen no sign of Appa. We all plopped down in the sand, depressed and hopeless. Then Katara started giving orders (she's good at that), telling us that if we didn't keep mov—ing, we were going to die. I could have told her that. Then as we made our way over a dune, I stubbed my toe on something.

Man, did that hurt. And boy, do I hate not being able to feel where I'm going! What was that thing, anyway? It feels like . . . huh? "What idiot buried a boat in the desert?"

"It's one of the gliders the Sandbenders use," Katara said. "And look, it's got some kind of compass. Aang, you can bend a breeze so we can sail it!"

Maybe our luck is starting to change. Maybe we'll make it out of the desert after all.

✤ ✤ ✤

We glided until we came to a giant rock cave. Katara hoped to find some water there. Aang hoped to find Sandbenders. Me? I'm just glad to get my feet back onto solid ground! Oh, this feels so good! I just have to stretch out and let my whole body come in contact with the rock.

But after a few seconds in the cave we started to hear strange sounds—of wings flapping and low buzzing. Suddenly we were surrounded by giant buzzard-wasps! They almost bit our heads off, but thankfully some Sandbenders came to our rescue. But even though they just saved us from the buzzard-wasps, I can tell that Aang's fury is growing.

Are these the Sandbenders who took Appa?

"What are you doing in our land with a sandsailer?" one of them asked. "From the looks of it, you stole it from the Hami tribe!"

"We're traveling with the Avatar," Katara explained. "Our bison was stolen, and we have to get to Ba Sing Se."

"You dare accuse our people of theft when you ride on a stolen sandsailer?" another Sandbender asked.

Wait a minute! I know that voice. That's the Sandbender who took Appa! I never forget a voice. I'm sure he's the one. No wonder he's overreacting. He's feeling guilty!

"Quiet, Ghashiun!" an older-sounding Sandbender shouted. "No one accused our people of anything."

"Sorry, Father."

"Aang," I whispered. "I recognize the son's voice. He's the one who stole Appa."

"Where is Appa? What did you do to him?" Aang suddenly yelled.

I've never seen Aang like this, not even when Appa was first taken—so enraged, so out of control. He just fired an Airbending blast that destroyed one of the sandsailers. I can feel the Sandbenders trembling nervously, but no one's saying or doing anything. And he just destroyed another one, even worse than he had the first. This is bad.

"Tell me where he is! Now!"

"It wasn't me!" Ghashiun cried.

"He's lying! I heard him tell the others to put a muzzle on Appa!" I'm not letting this kid get away with anything.

"I'm sorry!" Ghashiun finally cried. "I didn't know it belonged to the Avatar! I traded him to some nomads. He's probably in Ba Sing Se by now. They were going to sell him there."

Then the weirdest thing happened. Aang seemed to go into some kind of trance. I felt the wind whip up all around him, as if pure energy was radiating from his body. I was actually a bit scared, and I don't scare easily. But Katara was able to calm him down, and then he just collapsed in her arms, crying.

At least now we know where Appa is, except that it means we'll be going to Ba Sing Se, and I don't like that place.

Chapter 5

We're finally out of the desert and on our way to Ba Sing Se. Like I said, I don't like that city, but anything is better than the desert. Sokka studied a map he had taken from the spirit's library and discovered that there's only one way to get to there from where we are: by some thin strip of land called Serpent's Pass. Sounds creepy to me. . . .

On our way to Serpent's Pass we bumped into a family of refugees—a husband, his pregnant wife, and the wife's sister. They're also going to Ba Sing Se, and they told us about a ferry from a place called Full Moon

Bay that will take us there. They also told us Serpent's Pass is a deadly route.

Nice going, Sokka! Good choice.

We made it to Full Moon Bay, and we all got on line to buy tickets for the ferry.

The mean guard at the ticket counter won't sell Aang tickets because he, Sokka, and Katara don't have passports. I'm the only one with a passport, but I have a feeling that mine will be good enough for all of us. People just LOVE pleasing the Beifong family.

"I'll take care of this, Aang." Ha, I can't wait hear this guard's reaction. "My name is Toph Beifong and I'll need four tickets."

"Ah, the golden seal of the flying boar! It's my pleasure to help anyone of the Beifong family!"

See, it never fails! As much as I hated that stuffy mansion, there are times that being part of a wealthy, influential family has its advantages. This is one of those times.

While I was negotiating our entrance, Sokka ran into this girl Suki that he knows. She's one of the security officers, but she's also a Kyoshi warrior. And she OBVIOUSLY has a crush on him. Hmm. . . . I wonder if he feels the same way about her. He probably does. She feels all pretty and girly and light on her feet. Not that it really matters to me. I definitely don't care.

Just when I thought we were going to have a peaceful journey, the refugees told us their passports and tickets have just been stolen. Aang tried to talk to the ticket lady again, but she's not in the mood to listen. Now Aang's going to lead all of us through Serpent's Pass. So long quiet, peaceful boat ride. Hello, deadly pass.

🪙 🪙 🪙

Serpent's Pass is this thin ribbon of land with huge lakes on either side of it—these little adventures just keep getting worse. First, sand, which I can't bend; now, water, when I can't swim. . . . Oh, well, it's time to take the plunge. Our large group, including Suki and the refugee family, is starting to cross.

Sokka is being so annoying! He's all over Suki like that mother moose-lioness with her cub. "Are you sure you should be coming on this dangerous path, Suki?" "I wouldn't want anything to happen to you, Suki." "Don't sleep so close to that ledge, Suki. It may not be stable." Give me a break. I'm gonna barf. She's a warrior. I think she can take care of herself.

Whoa, a loud explosion just shook the path. I can feel an avalanche of rocks raining down from the side of the cliff above us!

"Fire Nation ships have spotted us!" Sokka shouted. He shoved Suki out of the way, but his move put him right in the path of the rocks.

Time to Earthbend a rock ledge above him. There, that'll protect him from the rocks. At least he's safe. And now he's dashing over to Suki, asking her if she's okay and telling her she needs to be more careful. Please! He's the one who should be careful—I just had to save HIS life! How about a little "thanks for saving my life, Toph." "Hey, no problem, Sokka, old buddy!" But no. He acts like I'm not even here. Whatever, I don't care. I don't need his thanks. Yuck—his fawning over Suki is so nauseating. How can she stand it? Okay, really, Toph, it's time to get over it. . . .

We just came to a spot where the path drops into the lake. Apparently there's a huge section of it that is completely covered with water. And I really can't swim! How am I going to get across?

"Everyone single file," Katara said.

Right! I'm traveling with a Waterbender.

Katara and Aang are lifting the water off the path, forming walls of water on either side of us. We're walking quickly through. I hate being so close to all this water, but I trust Katara. She'll get us across safely.

Just keep walking, Toph; soon you'll be away from all this water. What's that noise? I hear something snarling, and water's crashing down all around us. Time to switch it up with some Earthbending. . . . Here we go! Everyone up on my earth elevator. I'll just raise us above the splashing water; that should keep us safe from whatever it is. . . .

"It's a giant serpent!" Sokka cried. "I think I just figured out why they call it Serpent's Pass!"

Okay, well, I saved us from drowning, but now we're trapped on a tiny island of rock sticking out of the middle of the lake with a huge monster circling us! There's really no peace and quiet with this team, huh?

Katara just froze a strip of ice on the water's surface, connecting our little earth island to where the path resumes above the water level. It seems we're supposed to cross that while she and Aang jump into the water to battle the serpent with Waterbending and Airbending. I didn't think it could get worse than water and sand, but ice is worse than both. . . . This is awful! Wait, I can't feel anybody. Did everyone else cross already? So, I'm standing on this rock island, alone? I don't like this one bit.

"Toph, come on! It's just ice!"

Maybe it's just ice to you, Sokka, but to me it's a slippery surface I can't see or feel. Let me just put my toes on the ice and—No, no, I was right the first time. I'll just stay here on my little island. As long as that monster stays far away I—What's that crash? It's the serpent, and he's right behind me! Okay, that's it. No choice. Here I go. Here I go. I'm going. I'm—really—going! You did it! You're on the ice, just take little baby steps. Can't drift too far to the left or right or you'll end up in the lake.

"FOLLOW MY VOICE!" Sokka shouted.

As if it's that easy . . . okay, almost there,

almost—ahhhh! The serpent just smashed the ice bridge. "Help! I can't swim!"

"I'm coming, Toph!" I heard Sokka shout.

Surrounded by water . . . no sound, no sensation of touch. Total and complete isolation. Somebody better save me—quick! Oh, no! I'm sorry, Mom, Dad. I never meant to let you down. Maybe I shouldn't have left home. Maybe this whole freedom adventure thing was a big mistake. . . .

GASP. Strong arms . . . grabbing me . . . yanking me up! Ahhhh—air! I can breathe! Oh, Sokka! You saved me! Thank you, thank you. Sokka . . . my hero . . .

"Oh, Sokka, you saved me!"

I can't believe he dove in after me. This definitely deserves a kiss on the cheek, at least.

"Actually, it's me."

Oh, no. Is that Suki's voice? This can't be happening. I just made a complete fool of myself, didn't I? Getting all gushy over Sokka when the girl who really likes him is the one who saved me. Good move, Toph. Really slick.

"You can go ahead and let me drown now." Oh, why do I even care that he didn't rescue me anyway? I'm safe, right? That's all that matters, isn't it? I'm back on dry land, and Aang and Katara are safe too.

Our next stop is Ba Sing Se. Aang just flew off to start looking for Appa. Suki's going back to find her fellow Kyoshi warriors. But first she's sharing a tender good-bye scene with Sokka, complete with kissing. Yuck. It's nauseating to listen to. . . . It's kind of nice to be blind at moments like these. . . .

🪙 🪙 🪙

We made our way over to the base of Ba Sing Se's outer wall. But we were shocked to find Aang there.

"What are you doing here?" Katara asked. "I thought you were looking for Appa."

"I was. But something stopped me. Something big."

Time for another earth elevator. Up we go! Let's take a look for ourselves.

"It's a giant drill," Sokka said, "to cut through the outer wall of the city."

So, the Fire Nation's built a drill to break through the walls, and even the king's team of elite Earthbenders don't seem to be able to stop it. The city's in trouble. We need a plan.

"We'll take the drill down from the inside!" Sokka announced.

"By hitting its pressure points!" I added. Good idea, Sokka. You're actually not as big of a dud as you make yourself seem. . . .

"I'm going to give us some cover so we can sneak in," I told everyone. "Once I whip up some dust clouds, you're not going to be able to see, so stay close to me."

WHOOSH! "Run!"

Huh . . . this is one of the few times I can see and THEY can't. As long as I can still feel the ground with my feet, I'm golden. Okay, we're near the drill. Let me just open a hole in the ground and create a tunnel so we can get right up under it. Done.

"Everyone into the hole!"

"It's so dark down here," Sokka cried. "I can't see a thing!"

"Gee, Sokka, what a nightmare." Okay, I take it back. He IS a dud.

"There's an opening in the bottom of the drill," Sokka shouted. Aang's helping Katara and Sokka climb up into the drill.

No way I'm going in there! It's all metal. I can't bend metal, which means I'm blind in there. I'd be lost and useless. "I'll try to slow it down out here to give you more time."

Focus now. Concentrate, Toph, and . . . UP! If I can just jam this huge wedge of rock into the bottom of the drill to slow it down . . . Keep the energy coming. Keep it coming. It's too strong! It's pushing me backward. Come on, Toph, just dig your feet in, grab the ground. Ugh, my heels are digging up piles of earth behind me. I hope whatever they are doing in there, they're doing it fast!

It feels like I've been doing this for hours. The drill keeps creeping forward. I can't hold it anymore! I'm not doing any good here. I just wish there was something else I could—

Wait a minute! I hear voices down at the back end of the drill. Loud shrieking—I'd know those voices anywhere. It's Katara and Sokka arguing. But what are they doing back there? They're supposed to be inside the drill.

"You guys need some help?"

I found Sokka and Katara standing in what turned out to be a huge puddle of glop called slurry, a mixture of rock and water. Katara explained that it's been shooting through the drill and out an opening in the back end as it bore into the wall.

"Help me plug up this drain," Katara said. Together we bent the slurry back into the opening, to prevent it from pouring out.

So this stuff is SUPPOSED to come out. But, by trapping it inside, we are causing it to build up a lot of pressure. Whatever Aang is still doing in there, hopefully this will help him. We just have to keep pushing. Keep pushing. It's much easier working with Katara than try— ing to stop this monstrosity myself. Wait, I think it's time. It sounds like a tremendous crash is coming from the top of the drill.

"Here it comes!" This is so cool! The whole thing is lurching to the side, and slurry is exploding from every seam! Time to get out of the way. Up we go on another earth elevator . . . and there goes the slurry, gushing from the back of the drill.

I can hear the drill falling to pieces, and the motor is dead. It's finally over. We did it! We stopped the Fire Nation's drill!

Chapter 6

68 Now that that whole drill thing is over, we can finally start looking for Appa. So we're taking the train from the outer wall to the inner wall of Ba Sing Se. Everyone's excited to finally be in the city, but not me. Just when I was really enjoying the freedom of traveling, here we are back inside a city, trapped by a bunch of walls and rules. I have the same feeling I used to get back home. I know we have to find Appa and tell the king about the eclipse, but I'll be very happy when we finally get to leave this place.

We're finally at the station in the inner wall. I wonder how we're going to get around?

"Hello, my name is Joo Dee. I have the honor of showing the Avatar around Ba Sing Se. And you must be Sokka, Katara, and Toph."

Strange. This Joo Dee woman seems all nice and friendly, but she's so happy and bubbly and full of energy and good cheer. It's kind of creeping me out. How did she know that Aang was the Avatar? And how did she know the rest of our names, too? Who here knew we were coming?

"We have information about the Fire Nation that we need to deliver to the Earth King immediately," Sokka explained.

"Great!" Joo Dee replied in that sickeningly sweet voice. "Let's begin our tour."

She just completely blew Sokka off!

"Maybe you missed what I said. We need to talk to the king about the war. It's important."

"You're in Ba Sing Se now," she said. "Everyone is safe here."

How can she say that? We just saved them from a Fire Nation attack that could have brought down the entire city. I wish she knew how close she just came to becoming a pris-oner of the Fire Nation. Safe is the last thing she is. There is definitely something weird about this woman!

I've seen this kind of behavior before—from my parents and my teachers. It's called "being handled." It's when adults don't listen to what you say. They just tell you what they want you to hear. We're not even in the city one full day and already I'm sick of this place. Boy, oh boy, it's going to be a long visit, I can feel it. . . .

And she's insisting on taking us on a tour of the city.

"What's inside that oval wall?" Katara asked.

"And who are those mean—looking guys in robes?" Sokka added.

"That is the royal palace," Joo Dee explained. "And those men are agents of the Dai Li. They are the guardians of all our traditions."

"Can we see the king now?" Aang blurted out.

Good for you, Aang. I'm tired of tiptoeing around this lady.

"Oh, no! One doesn't just pop in on the king. But your request to see the king is being processed, and should be put through in about a month! Much more quickly than usual!"

Is she for real? No way I'm staying in this place for a whole month!

🀄 🀄 🀄

Joo Dee showed us to our house, but none of us were in the mood to relax. So we decided to walk through town searching for Appa. Joo Dee insisted on coming with us.

Unfortunately we've had no luck. No one has seen Appa, and no one even wants to talk to us. I don't think I'm going to survive here if everyone acts this way. It's so frustrating. It's like there's a big secret here that everyone's hiding and we're the only ones who don't know it!

🀄 🀄 🀄

It's our second day in Ba Sing Se, and I'm hoping today is going to be better than yesterday. Katara actually came up with a plan for us to see the king, so tonight Katara and I are getting all dressed up in fancy clothes and makeup, so we can sneak into a party the king is throwing. It's a perfect opportunity to tell him about our information!

At first the guards at the door wouldn't let us in, but then this guy Long Feng helped us get in. Then he wouldn't leave us alone until we found our "families." We were finally able to lose him. We were supposed to let Aang and Sokka in through the back door, but somehow Aang and Sokka snuck in without our help. Anyway, we're all inside now. Time to set the plan in motion.

"What are you doing here? You have to leave, or we'll all be in terrible trouble!"

That voice, it's so familiar. It's Joo Dee! We just can't get rid of her. But we can't let her stop us when we've gotten this far.

"Keep their attention while I find the Earth King," Sokka said to Aang.

Come on, Aang, just keep their attention until someone spots the king—Ahhhh! Who's grabbing me? Where are we going? This is not good. We're obviously not wanted here. I guess we're getting a little too close to whatever big secret makes this place so mysterious and makes everyone who lives here so frightened.

"Why won't you let us talk to the king?" Sokka shouted. "We have information that could defeat the Fire Nation!"

At least everyone is here with me. I wonder

who these guys are, and what they will do to us.

"The Earth King has no time to get involved with political squabbles and the day-to-day minutia of military activities," a man said.

It's that Long Feng guy. He's the cultural minister to the king and head of the Dai Li. What a liar! I bet he knew exactly who we were when he met us. And what kind of answer is that? What else could the king possibly be concerned with?

"But this could be the most important thing he's ever heard," Aang said.

"What's important to the king is maintaining the cultural heritage of Ba Sing Se," Long Feng shot back. "It's my job to oversee the rest of the city's resources, including the military."

"So the king is just a figurehead," Katara said.

Even though Long Feng's denying it, it's pretty obvious to me what's going on here. Long Feng has the power. He controls the city. And he keeps the king in the dark.

"You can't keep the truth from the people of the city!" Katara shouted. "They have to know."

"I'll tell them," Aang added. "I'll make sure everyone knows."

"I understand you've been looking for your bison," Long Feng retorted. "It would be a shame if you were not able to complete your quest."

Does this guy know where Appa is? I can feel Aang getting angrier by the second. And now I know that it's a really bad idea to make Aang mad.

Long Feng finally let us go. But as we were leaving, a woman came into the room and introduced herself as Joo Dee. But she's not the Joo Dee we know. She's someone completely different, claiming she's Joo Dee. Seriously, this city just keeps getting weirder and weirder. And I just keep liking it less and less.

Chapter 7

We've been putting posters up all around town, asking if anyone has seen Appa, but no one has. We've finally decided to take a break and return home. That's when Joo Dee—the original Joo Dee, not the second one—knocked on our door.

"What happened to you?" Sokka asked. "Did the Dai Li throw you into jail?"

"Of course not," she said. "I simply took a short vacation to Lake Laogai."

"Why are you here?" Aang asked.

"Putting up posters is not permitted. It's against the rules."

"We don't care about the rules!" Aang yelled. "We're finding Appa on our own, and you should just stay out of our way."

All right, Aang! I've been wanting to say that since I set foot in this place. Time to break some rules!

🪙 🪙 🪙

So we headed back out. While we were putting up posters, Katara ran into this kid named Jet that she knows from before. I don't know what he did to her in the past, but she's really mad at him.

"Katara, I swear I've changed," he pleaded. "I don't even have my gang now. I've put all that behind me. I'm here to help you find Appa."

"You're lying!"

Hmm, that's odd. I can feel his heartbeat and the vibrations his body's making as he breathes in and out. He's feels perfectly calm. His breathing is normal and his heart rate is steady. If he was lying, his heart rate would speed up and his breathing would grow faster and unsteady. No, this guy is telling the truth. "He's not lying."

🪙 🪙 🪙

Even though Katara is still skeptical, we've decided to follow Jet to this warehouse where he heard they were keeping Appa.

This place is empty! Appa's certainly not here. Maybe Katara is right about this guy. Maybe he's leading us into a trap. Maybe— Wait a minute. What's that? I'm stepping in something that feels very familiar. It feels like— oh. "Appa was here," I announced, reaching down, picking up a handful of his fur.

"We missed him," Aang said sadly.

"They took that big thing to Whale-tail Island—very, very far from here," said an unknown voice. Apparently the building janitor has seen Appa. Aang's insisting we go, no matter how far away it is. Jet said he'll help, but Katara still doesn't trust him.

Boy, oh boy, is she steamed up! Her heart is pounding like a hammer and her breathing is all over the place. Katara really likes this guy! "Was he your boyfriend or something?"

"No!"

Ha! She's totally lying. No wonder she's so mad at him.

As we got ready to leave, two people came

running over to Jet. They seem to know him.

"How did you get away from the Dai Li?" one of them asked him. Then she turned to Katara. "He got arrested by the Dai Li a couple of weeks ago."

"I don't know what she's talking about," Jet insisted.

Okay, now this is really weird. Impossible, in fact. The girl who's saying that Jet had been arrested, and Jet, who's insisting that he hadn't been, are BOTH telling the truth. Normal heart rates and breathing in both of them. How can that be?

"They both THINK they're telling the truth," Sokka discovered, "which means that Jet has been brainwashed!"

I guess he's not such a dud after all. That makes sense, finally.

"The Dai Li must have sent Jet to mislead us, and that janitor was part of their plot too," Katara said.

"I bet they have Appa right here in the city," Aang said excitedly. "Maybe they took him to the same place they took Jet. We need to find a way to jog his real memories."

So Katara's Waterbending a sparkling band of healing energy around Jet's head. Slowly he's beginning to relax. Soon his true memories are going to drift up through the brainwashing . . . and here it comes. Apparently, the Dai Li had taken him to their headquarters, underwater, beneath a lake.

"Joo Dee said she went on a vacation to Lake Laogai," Sokka recalled.

"That's it!" Jet cried. "Lake Laogai!"

Okay, now he's DEFINITELY telling the truth. I hope Appa's there, I really do. I can't wait to put this whole Appa mess behind me. If he's really gone, I don't know what I'll do.

We've finally arrived at Lake Laogai, but there's no sign of any kind of headquarters. There's nothing here. It's just a lake and— Whoa, wait a second! It's hollow beneath this rock! That's an entrance!

"Got it!" I shouted. I'll just Earthbend this rock up and—there it is, a tunnel leading under the lake. Okay, we're heading down now. It feels huge. . . .

"I think there might be a cell big enough to hold Appa up ahead," Jet said.

Again he's telling the truth. Please be in there, Appa. Please!

Okay, we're in and—

"Take them into custody!"

Long Feng! But Jet was telling the truth! He expected to find Appa here. Oh, well, it looks like instead of finding Appa we're going to be fighting Dai Li agents.

They're pretty good Earthbenders—very good, in fact. But nothing I can't handle, especially with help from the others. Is that all you got, Dai Li? You guys wouldn't even make it through Earth Rumble Six! You just—Oh, no! Aang said Long Feng's escaping!

Good, Aang and Jet are on it. Katara, Sokka, and I can finish up these Dai Li wimps.

🉑 🉑 🉑

By the time we caught up to Aang and Jet in the other room, Jet was lying on the ground. No sign of Long Feng, but things aren't looking so good for Jet. Katara's trying to heal him, but I can't tell if it's working. He's telling Katara that he'll be fine, but the sad thing is, this time, it feels like he's lying.

Back out into the tunnels. Focus, Toph, feel the spaces behind the doors. No, too small to hold Appa. Too small. Too—here it is! Behind that door. If he's in this tunnel he's in that room. In we go and—empty!

"He's gone!" Aang cried. "Long Feng beat us here."

"If we keep moving, maybe we can catch up with them!" Sokka said.

These tunnels are like mazes. Got to feel for the twists and turns and—the stairs! Here's the way back up! "Come on! Follow me!"

Finally, we made it—back out onto the shore. And we're surrounded by Dai Li troops—lots of them! Too many, from the feel of it. We can't take them all. I can't believe we came all this way and we didn't even find Appa. I can barely face Aang. I can only imagine what he must be feeling. This is all my fault.

Wait, what's Momo doing? He's chirping wildly like he knows something.

"Appa!" Aang shouted.

Appa's back! Yup, I'd know that unmistakable thud anywhere—even in the sand! I don't know how, but he's back. After Aang, I think I'm the most relieved person in the world.

🀄 🀄 🀄

It didn't take Appa long to Airbend the Dai Li troops into the lake with his huge tail. Then he bit Long Feng on the leg and tossed him into the water too.

As uncomfortable as I am being off the ground and on Appa's back, I've never been so happy to climb up onto the big, smelly beast. Welcome back, Appa. Welcome back.

🀄 🀄 🀄

Now that we have Appa there's nothing stopping us from telling the Earth King the truth about the war, the eclipse, and Long Feng's conspiracy for power. Well, almost nothing— except a bunch of royal Earthbending guards at the king's palace! We just have to keep battling our way in. . . .

Finally! We're face-to-face with the king in his throne room. Long Feng and some Dai Li agents are here too. Surprise, surprise.

"We need to talk to you!" Aang insisted.

"He's lying!" Long Feng shouted. "They're here to overthrow you."

"You invade my palace, lay waste to my guards, and you expect me to trust you?"

"He has a good point," I said.

But when he heard that Aang is the Avatar, the king decided to listen to us.

"There's a war going on right now—for the last hundred years, in fact," Aang explained. "The Dai Li's kept it secret from you. It's a conspiracy to control the city and to control you!"

After a lot of coaxing, the king agreed to allow us to prove our point. So we're taking him to Lake Laogai to show him the Dai Li's secret headquarters.

Okay, where's that entrance? Wait a minute. How can this be? Still, I can feel it with my feet. "It's gone! There's nothing down there anymore."

"The Dai Li must have destroyed the evidence," Katara said.

Great. Now the king will never believe us! Not that I blame him. I mean, our evidence doesn't exist anymore. But now Katara's pleading with him to come back and look at Ba Sing Se's outer wall. Hey, I know what she's going for here—great idea! She wants to show him the Fire Nation drill! There's still a chance. . . .

We're heading back toward the wall—there's the drill, right where we destroyed it! The king has to believe us now. . . .

"Dai Li, arrest Long Feng!" the king ordered.

Whoo hoo! He finally believes us. Now we're getting somewhere.

🜨 🜨 🜨

We were back in the throne room when a general named How arrived with some amazing news.

"We searched Long Feng's office," he said. "I think we've found something that will interest everybody. Secret files on everyone in Ba Sing Se, including you kids."

"It's a letter from your mom, Toph," Katara said. "She's here in the city, and she wants to see you!"

Wow! I can't believe my mom's here! I never thought she'd defy my father. . . . I thought my leaving would be the end of our relationship. But I guess Iroh's nephew, Zuko, isn't the only lucky one. . . . I guess my mother cares too.

I handed Katara the letter and asked her to read it to me.

It sounds like she's changed—a lot. Like she finally understands who I really am, and she's ready to accept me. This is almost too good to be true. For the first time in a long time, I really can't wait to see her!

Everybody else got good news too. Aang was given a scroll found on Appa's horn, telling him about a guru at the Eastern Air Temple who can help him with the Avatar state. And Katara and Sokka found out where their dad's Water Tribe fleet is.

It looks like we're all going our separate ways. Aang and Sokka are flying off on Appa—Sokka's going to find his dad, and Aang's off to find his guru. Katara is staying behind with the king. And I'm off to meet my mom.

🉐 🉐 🉐

I can't believe how sad I am that we're splitting up. These guys have definitely had an impact on me. I was wrong, thinking I could always do everything on my own. I need these guys. They're my friends. And I'm really, really going

85

to miss them. But I can't pass up a chance to see my mom. Besides, we'll meet up again, I know it.

⊕ ⊕ ⊕

I'm off to this fancy apartment building where my mom's supposed to be waiting for me. Okay, here's the apartment, just breathe. It's going to be fine. She wants to see you, right? After all, she wrote that letter. She reached out and traveled all this distance. It's going to be better than fine. It's going to be great. Just stay calm.

KNOCK. KNOCK.

"Hello, Mom?"

KNOCK. KNOCK. That's odd. The door just swung open. "Anyone home?" Hmm . . . I guess I should go in.

"Hello!"

Something's very wrong here. This apart—ment is empty! There's no furniture. There's nothing here at all.

WHAM!

What's that? Something just dropped over me from above, surrounding me on all sides. Some kind of cage . . . a cage that I can't bend! It must be made of metal! "Who's here? And who do you think you're dealing with?"

"One loud—mouthed, little brat who's strayed too far from home."

I know that voice. It's Xin Fu from the Earth-bending arena!

How did he find me? He must have followed me all the way from home. So much for the loving, teary reunion with my mother. The letter, it was just a fake, a hoax, just to get me here. How could I be so stupid to think my mother would come all this way to tell me that she now understood me?

The cage is being lifted. I must be on some kind of platform. No, it's a carriage—with an ostrich—horse, by the sound and smell of it.

And now we're moving! I'm trapped. I wonder if the others are in trouble too? I don't know how, but I've got to get out of this cage! I've got to find my friends!

Chapter 8

88 We've been traveling for hours, I'm sure of it. But since I can't bend metal, I can't sense the vibrations of the ground or trees around me, and so I have no idea where we are. But from the sounds, the smell, and the bumpy ride, I think we're in a forest.

"I believe we need to go right."

THAT'S not Xin Fu, it's Master Yu! So he's in on this too.

"What are you talking about," Xin Fu replied. "The Beifong's estate is this way."

Hmm. Maybe I can use this to my advantage.

"Hey! Can you two old ladies quit bickering

for a second? I have to go to the bathroom!"

"Okay, but make it quick," Master Yu said.

"What's wrong with you?" Xin Fu shouted.

Great. NOW he's got brains!

"Very sneaky, Toph!" Master Yu said, trying to sound like he wasn't fooled. "Nice try, but you can't fool me."

"You may think you're the greatest Earthbender in the world, but even you can't bend metal!" Xin Fu added in his smug tone.

I need to get out of here! If only I COULD bend metal, I'd be out of here in a minute. Then those guys would be—

Wait a minute . . . metal comes from the earth. If I can bend it when it's still ore embedded deep in rocks, why shouldn't I be able to bend it in its processed form? It's the same stuff, right? Maybe it's not the METAL that's holding me prisoner, it's my mind. Sheesh. Now I'm starting to sound like Aang!

But what if it's true? Aang always had the power to Earthbend within him. It was only his approach that stopped him. Maybe that's my problem too. Okay. Here we go.

Hands against the back wall of the cage.

Focus, Toph. Focus. Go back to day one, the first time you ever moved a rock. Remember, that seemed so hard until you found the right place in your mind, the right level of concentration. After that, it was a snap.

Come on, metal, bend, bend! Nothing. Okay, deep breath, then try again.

Bend, metal. You can't hold me back. You can't box in willpower. I am rooted. I am solid. You will bend!

My hands are trembling. I can feel power surging from deep within me. The metal is starting to buckle. Yes! Toph, you rule! Okay, okay, don't get carried away. Take that feeling and build on it. Focus. Harder, harder. Push!

The back wall of the cage is ripping open. I'm free! I'm out of that cage! And I've gained a whole new Earthbending skill in the bargain.

I'll just slip around to the front of the carriage and give those clowns a surprise.

"What was that noise?" Master Yu asked.

"It must be one of her tricks," Xin Fu replied.

"It's no trick," I said, standing right beside them. "And neither is this."

WHOOSH! Take that, you clowns! Now it's your turn in the cage. I'll just Metalbend the cage shut—I love this! There, now you're trapped. How does it feel, boys? "I AM the greatest Earthbender in the world. And don't you two dunderheads ever forget it!"

🜰 🜰 🜰

Finally—free again! I'll just ride this Earthwave back toward Ba Sing Se. Freedom tastes especially sweet today, knowing that there is now one less element that can hold me!

Too bad about that letter, though. Too bad it wasn't real. It would be really great if my folks could understand and accept me. Yeah, like that's ever going to happen.

Wheeee! This is the only way to fly—with my feet still on the ground! Man, Earthwave riding is the best. Once I get there, I've got to see if Katara and the others are all right. I mean, if the letter from my mom is a fake, who knows about Katara's dad and Aang's guru. I—

Whoa! What's that! Something swooping down from the sky. I'm losing the wave! I'm crashing down—

BOOM! Appa? "Hey! Don't sneak up on me like that!"

"Need a ride?"

Sokka's here too! I guess I'll be riding Appa the rest of the way—oh, joy.

On our way back Aang told me that while he was with the guru, he had a vision that Katara was in trouble. That's why he left. He picked up Sokka on the way. Gosh, I hope that Katara's okay. I hope Aang's vision isn't real. . . .

We're back at our house in Ba Sing Se, but Katara isn't home.

"Katara IS in trouble," Aang said. "I knew it!"

And now I can feel someone else is coming. "Someone's at the door." I recognize the footfall. "Actually, I know who it is. It's an old friend of mine." I flung the door open, and sure enough, it's Iroh.

"I need your help."

"You know each other?" Aang asked.

"I met him in the woods once, and knocked him down. Then he gave me tea and some very good advice."

I invited him in. Sokka immediately took up a warrior's stance. "I'm warning you. If you make one false move . . ."

Give him a break, Sokka. This guy seems about as dangerous as a soggy tea leaf.

"Princess Azula is in Ba Sing Se," the old man began.

"She must have Katara!" Aang said.

"She has captured my nephew as well."

"Then we'll work together to fight Azula, and save Katara and Zuko," Aang said.

The old man brought along a Dai Li agent he had captured. Intimidated by a bunch of angry benders, the guy talked right away. "Azula and Long Feng are plotting a coup. They're going to overthrow the Earth King."

"Where are they keeping Katara?" Sokka insisted.

"In the crystal catacombs of Old Ba Sing Se, deep beneath the palace!"

I wasn't here to help Katara before. But I'm going to help her now. I'm going to find those catacombs.

We're hurrying to the palace courtyard. Hmm . . . I can't feel anything. Everything seems pretty solid. "If there's an ancient city down there, it's deep." I'll just blast them open. Yup, the catacombs are definitely down there.

"We should split up," Sokka suggested. "Aang, you go with Iroh to look for Katara and the angry jerk. No offense . . ."

"None taken," Iroh replied.

"And I'll go with Toph to warn the king about Azula's coup."

✦ ✦ ✦

Okay, we're close to the palace; the Dai Li is arresting General How!

"The coup is happening right now!", Sokka said. "We've got to warn the Earth King!"

We're in the throne room. Something feels strange to me. Huh? Who's that? Feels like a Kyoshi warrior. And she's heading right for Sokka. If Suki thinks we have time for smooches, she's sorely mistaken. . . .

"Hi, cutie," she cooed.

Wait a minute—that's not Suki! And that's a voice I've heard before. "They're not the real Kyoshi warriors!"

Oh, boy, I can feel darts heading right at me! I'll raise a stone slab. This is crazy. I mean, I like bending just as much as the next person, but when will this madness stop!

"This fight is over."

Azula! And it sounds like she's standing right next to the king. She's right. The fight is over. We can't risk endangering the king. One quick fire blast from her and the king would be seriously hurt. We have to give up. . . .

🏵 🏵 🏵

So, Azula's Dai Li agents led me, Sokka, Momo, and the Earth King out of the throne room, and have locked us in what they called an "Earthbender-proof" prison cell. In other words, it's made out of metal.

Beautiful! I love surprising the bad guys. This is one of those times I'm sad I'm blind . . . I have to miss out on seeing their shocked faces!

Here you go, Toph, you can do this again. Channel the energy . . . NOW!

The metal cell door is open. Time to make a dash for the entrance to the tunnel. Almost there, almost—Wait, someone's heading toward us. It's Katara! But where's Aang?

Oh, no! He's hurt! She's carrying him.

Just then Appa swept down and picked us up—me, Sokka, Katara, Momo, the Earth King, the king's pet bear, and Aang, stretched out motionless on Appa's soft fur.

Katara's using her healing water to revive him. His eyes are open! Oh, thank goodness!

But, you know, I wonder if any of us is really going to be okay. I mean, the Earth Kingdom has fallen to Azula and the Fire Nation. Now what do we do? We thought we were doing the right thing, we thought delivering that message would make everything all right. We thought it would end the war..

But now that hope is gone. Azula has control of the Earth Kingdom, and once again we're on the run. Don't get me wrong, I wouldn't want to be on the run with any other team. I'm glad I met Sokka, Katara, and Aang—even Appa and Momo.

But what happens next? I wish someone had the answer, because I have no idea. I guess I'll just do what I always do: feel my way through and hope for the best.

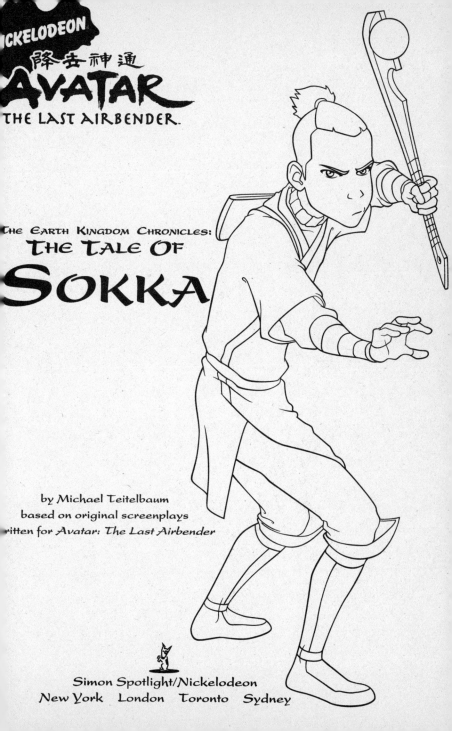

NICKELODEON

降去神通
AVATAR
THE LAST AIRBENDER.

THE EARTH KINGDOM CHRONICLES:
THE TALE OF
SOKKA

by Michael Teitelbaum
based on original screenplays
written for *Avatar: The Last Airbender*

Simon Spotlight/Nickelodeon
New York   London   Toronto   Sydney

Chapter 1

My name is Sokka. I'm a warrior from the Southern Water Tribe. My sister, Katara, and I have been traveling with Aang, the Avatar, for some time now. We're kind of his unofficial bodyguards. Katara is a Waterbender and she's been teaching Aang Waterbending. As a master of planning strategy, I'm here for my brains—and for my skill in battle with a boomerang.

We've just stopped a Fire Nation attack on the Water Tribes of the North Pole. Okay, so Aang really did most of the actual stopping, but Katara and I were right there to give our support.

While we were at the North Pole I met the most amazing girl in the world, Princess Yue. She was beautiful. And I say "was" because she became the moon to help save the Water Tribe. It was so sad. I was SO sad. . . . But she did the right thing.

Well, enough mushy stuff! I've got a job to do.

Aang has to travel to the Earth Kingdom next to begin learning Earthbending from his old pal King Bumi in the Earth Kingdom city of Omashu. You see, Aang has to master all four elements so he can stop the Fire Nation and end the war that's messed up the lives of so many people—including mine. My dad left home with other warriors from the Southern Water Tribe to fight the Fire Nation. Katara and I haven't seen him in a very long time, and I really, really miss him.

Aang, Katara, Momo (Aang's winged lemur), and I all climbed onto Appa (Aang's flying bison) and flew off toward Omashu. Our first stop was an Earth Kingdom base run by General Fong. This Fong guy was supposed to provide us with an escort to Omashu.

"Welcome, Avatar Aang!" Fong said when

we landed. "And welcome to all of you, great heroes. Appa, Momo, mighty Katara, and brave Sokka."

Now THIS guy had things figured out. He called me "brave Sokka!" Awesome.

But Fong had a strange idea: He wanted to force Aang into the Avatar state—where he gets amazingly powerful, but a little out of control—so he could defeat the Fire Lord quickly. Aang agreed with the general, but Katara didn't.

"Aang, there's a right way to do this," she said. "Practice, study, discipline."

That sounded pretty dull to me. "Or just glow it up and stomp that Fire Lord!" I countered.

"Katara, I don't have time to do this the right way!" Aang said.

Glow it up, here we come! But no matter how hard Fong tried, Aang just couldn't force himself into the Avatar state. And Fong went all nutso about it! He slammed Aang with an Earthbending blast, knocking him through a window! I couldn't believe this guy had just attacked Aang.

Before I could do anything, Fong's soldiers grabbed me, which made me even madder. I struggled to break free of the soldiers' grasp, then rushed to help Aang.

At that moment, Fong made the ground in the courtyard open up and swallow Katara.

"Katara! No!" I called out.

That's when Aang's fury made him slip into the Avatar state. Come on, buddy, you've got to rescue Katara!

He whipped up a huge funnel of wind that knocked aside Fong and his soldiers. Boy, Aang is really scary looking when he's like that.

"Katara is really in no danger," Fong admitted. "Burying her in the ground was just a trick to get Aang mad."

Well it sure worked! And just like that, Katara was freed. But Fong wasn't satisfied. That guy was really out of his mind.

"That was almost perfect!" he shouted as Katara comforted Aang. "We just have to find a way to control you when you're like that. I guess we'll figure it out on the way to the Fire Nation."

Uh-uh. There was no way the general was coming with us to the Fire Nation. As far as I was concerned, the only place he was going to was dreamland.

I sneaked up behind Fong and bopped him on the helmet with my boomerang.

WAP! Down he went for a nice little nap.

"Anybody got a problem with that?" I asked, looking around at Fong's troops. Not surprisingly, no one protested.

Next stop, Omashu!

We stopped by a river for a short rest.

From out of nowhere I heard music. Looking up I saw a group of weird-looking people coming from the woods. They played musical instruments and sang. Hmm . . . they seemed friendly, but these days you never know. The Fire Nation is tricky and they've got lots of spies everywhere. I wouldn't put it past them to be working in disguise to throw us off.

I confronted these so-called musicians. "Who are you?"

"I'm Chong, and this is my wife, Lily," said a guy with long hair and flowers around his neck. "We're nomads, happy to go wherever the wind takes us."

Nomads, huh? Could be. But how would we know for sure?

"I'm a nomad too," Aang said.

"Hey, me too!" Chong replied.

"I know. You just said that," Aang said.

Okay, so they couldn't be spies. The guy seemed too out of it to be from the Fire Nation!

Chong started telling Aang stories about all the places he'd been. While that's all very nice, we had someplace we needed to be. "Look, I hate to be the wet blanket here, but we need to get to Omashu quickly. No sidetracks," I said.

"Omashu is dangerous. Maybe you should go someplace else," Chong chimed in.

What's with this guy? We're not tourists looking for a fun vacation spot. We're on a mission. A very important mission. "We're going to Omashu!" I repeated.

"Whoa! Sounds like someone's got a case of destination fever. You worry too much about where you're going."

Maybe he didn't hear me right, so I repeated, louder this time, "O-MA-SHU!"

Then Katara explained that we needed to find King Bumi so that Aang could learn Earthbending.

"Sounds like you guys are headed to Omashu," Chong said, like it was the first time he had heard of our plan.

I smacked my forehead in frustration. "That's what I've been trying to tell you all along!" This guy was really dense.

Then Chong told us about a secret tunnel that leads right through the mountain. A short—cut to Omashu carved by two lovers who were the first Earthbenders.

"I think we'll just stick with flying," I said. "We've dealt with the Fire Nation before. We'll be fine."

We took off on Appa, but a few minutes into our flight the Fire Nation attacked, shooting huge fireballs at us and trying to knock us from the sky. Okay, this was way more than we'd faced before. And Appa was freaking out from the fire. We had to turn back. "Secret tunnel, here we come!"

"Actually, it's not just one tunnel," Chong told us when we returned to the river. "It's a whole labyrinth."

"A labyrinth?" I asked. A series of twisting paths built so that anyone who entered would get hopelessly lost inside forever? Great plan, Chong! Maybe those fireballs weren't that hot after all.

"It'll be fun, Sokka," Aang said, smiling that cheery, optimistic smile he always has.

Fun? Oh, sure, getting lost in an endless maze, being stuck in the dark, and being trapped with no food is definitely my idea of a good time! Not.

At that moment I spotted smoke in the sky. "It's the Fire Nation. They're tracking us. Everyone into the tunnels," I said.

The nomads lit five torches so we could find our way in the dark. Now it was up to me. I'm the plan guy. All we needed was a plan. "Chong, how long do those torches last?"

"Two hours each."

"We have five torches, so that means we have ten hours of light!" Lily said.

I smacked my forehead again. These nomads sure were completely clueless. I tried to be patient as I explained, "It doesn't work like that if they're all lit at the same time!"

Suddenly a wolf–bat came flying right at Katara. I swung my torch at the creature, but the torch slipped from my hand and rolled toward Appa.

The fire freaked Appa out and he started jumping around and slamming his tail into the wall. Unfortunately, the force of Appa's tail shook loose rocks from the ceiling, and they came tumbling down all around us.

The next thing I knew I was flying backward through the air. When I landed, I saw that a huge wall of rock had fallen between me and Aang, Katara, and Appa. Aang must have pushed me to safety with an Airbending blast.

Oh, boy, now I was trapped on the side of the rock wall with Momo and those annoying singing nomads! I began pulling rocks off the pile, trying to break through.

"It's no use," Chong said. "We're separated. But at least you have us."

"Noooo!" I was not going to spend whatever time was left in my life with those smiling, singing, clueless nomads! I picked up my pace, digging though the rocks faster and faster, but all I succeeded in doing was bringing more rocks down from above. It was no use. I had to find another way out.

As we moved further through the tunnels, the nomads began singing, "Don't let the cave-in get you down . . ."

"I don't get it," I said. "You guys travel around the world with no maps and no idea of where you're going. How do you ever get anywhere?"

"Somewhere is everywhere, and so you never really need to get anywhere because you're already here," Chang said.

"Don't remind me," I said, almost ready to admit defeat. I know I'm here! That's the problem. I don't want to be here, I want to be there, which is where I'm not. Oh, great—I was starting to sound like them.

That's when I heard wolf-bats howl again.

We kept moving, but I was completely lost. It was strange. I had a feeling the tunnels were constantly changing, because once again we hit a dead end. But how could they be changing?

"Your plans have led us to a dead end," said a nomad named Moku.

"At least I'm trying to get us out of here!" I replied impatiently.

Then a flock of wolf-bats swarmed us. I

swatted at the bats with my boomerang, but amazingly they all just flew right past us.

"Sokka, you saved us!" Chong said.

"No, they didn't leave because of me," I said, realizing what was happening. "They were fleeing."

"Fleeing? From what?"

A low roar filled the caves. "From whatever is making that noise!"

Suddenly the cave wall burst open and giant badger—moles rushed out.

I was right! The tunnels were changing because the badger—moles were digging new ones all the time. But being right didn't do much good if I wasn't going to make it out of there to tell anyone.

As one humongous creature came at me, I tripped and fell backward. My hand hit the strings of one of the nomad's instruments and it made a musical sound, which caused a very strange thing to happen: The badger—mole stopped charging and actually looked friendly.

Badger—moles. Music. Digging. That's it! Sokka's got a plan!

"Quick, start playing," I shouted to the nomads. "Play anything, as long as it's music!"

They made up a song about the badger—moles, but it really didn't make any difference what they were singing about. As long as they made music, the badger—moles stayed friendly. So friendly, in fact, that they let us climb up onto their backs as they tunneled through the mountain.

A while later, with me leading and the nomads singing, the badger—moles burst

through the far side of the mountain.

We made it—we were out! The nomads turned out to be good for something after all.

Aang, Katara, and Appa were waiting for us. "How did you guys get out?" I asked.

"Like the legend says, we let love lead the way," Aang said.

Okay, that sounds corny, but whatever. "Really? We let huge ferocious beasts lead our way," I bragged.

"Why is your forehead all red?" Katara asked me, but I didn't explain.

"Nobody react to what I'm about to tell you,"

Chong whispered as he pointed at Aang. "I think that kid might be the Avatar."

I slapped my forehead in disbelief one more time, and Katara understood why it was red.

We said our good-byes and continued on our way to Omashu. As we reached the top of a hill I pulled out my telescope to get my first look at the great Earth Kingdom city.

"I present to you the Earth Kingdom city of O—Oh, no!" I couldn't believe what I was seeing. A huge Fire Nation flag was hanging from the city's main wall. How could this have happened? How could the Fire Nation have taken over Omashu? And what about King Bumi?

Our journey just got a whole lot tougher.

Chapter 2

What do we do now?

Aang was really upset. "Omashu always seemed untouchable," he said.

"Up until now it was," I said. "Now Ba Sing Se is the only great Earth Kingdom stronghold left."

"This is horrible," Katara said, "but we have to move on."

"No," Aang insisted.

"There are other people who can teach you Earthbending, Aang," she pointed out.

"This isn't about finding a teacher. It's about finding my friend."

Hard to argue with that, but we still had one little problem. How did we get inside? We couldn't exactly stroll into an occupied city and ask to see the king, who may or may not still be in power.

That's when Aang found a secret passageway. Actually, it was a filthy, slime–ridden sewer. Aang opened the entrance and a wave of thick, green muck came pouring out.

Oh, man, it was the most disgusting thing I've ever smelled! I thought I was going to be sick.

Aang used Airbending to create a bubble for us to walk in as we made our way along the sewer pipe, but for some reason I still came out completely covered in stinky muck at the other end.

The things I have to do to win a war.

We popped out of a manhole on a quiet street in the city and I could barely breathe. Katara washed the muck off me with a Waterbending move, then Aang dried me off with an Airbending wind. That's when I noticed the little round, purple bug–type things attached to my face. "I'm doomed!" I yelled. "Some horrible poisonous sewer bugs are sucking the brains from my head! Help! Get them off! Ahh!"

"Stop making so much noise," Aang scolded, reaching out for one of the bugs. "It's just a purple pentapus."

Aang gently tickled one of the hideous leeches with his finger and it let go. As he was freeing the creatures, a group of Fire Nation soldiers showed up. Uh—oh.

"What are you kids doing out past curfew?" one of them asked.

Curfew? The Fire Nation has imposed a curfew on the city? This was horrible. I struggled to come up with a good answer fast, but Katara beat me to it.

"We were just on our way home," she replied.

Not great, but at least it's an answer.

Then a Fire Nation soldier pointed at me and asked, "What's the matter with him?"

What? What did he mean? What's wrong with me? What was he talking about?

"He has pentapox, sir," Katara said. "That's what those spots are on his face."

Spots? On my face? What is SHE talking about?

"It's highly contagious," Katara continued.

I finally got it. Those purple whatchamacallits

must have left spots on my face. It was time for a little acting.

"It's so awful!" I moaned in my best sick-guy voice. I can be a great actor. "I'm dying! Dying!"

"It's also deadly," Katara added.

Now for a little more moaning and coughing. Ah, the soldiers have taken off! They're scared. Pentapox. Good one, Katara. And not a bad performance on my part, either.

We continued along the streets. It was weird. Last time we were here this was a busy city with people everywhere. Now it's like a ghost town. Must be the curfew.

Then from out of nowhere a family came strolling down the empty street, guarded by more Fire Nation soldiers. They must be important people. Just before I could figure out who they were, a low rumbling noise filled the air.

I looked up and saw large boulders rolling down Omashu's mail chutes, heading straight for the family, which included a teenage girl and a young boy.

Aang moved quickly, Airbending the boulders away from the family. To our surprise, the woman cried out, "The resistance!"

The teenage daughter immediately began flinging flying daggers at Aang—at all of us, in fact! What a way to show gratitude.

So the good news was that there must be some kind of organized resistance to the Fire Nation's takeover of the city. The bad news was that the girl with the special daggers thought we were part of it! And she's got good aim!

It was time to run!

As a dozen flying daggers zipped our way, the ground beneath us suddenly began to drop, and then stopped abruptly. We fell to the ground, and when I rubbed the dust out of my eyes I saw that we were underground, surrounded by a bunch of Earth Kingdom people. These guys were the resistance. They saved us.

"So is King Bumi with you guys?" Aang asked. "Is he leading the resistance?"

The look of surprise on everyone's faces was unexpected.

"Of course not," the resistance leader said. "On the day of the invasion King Bumi surrendered."

He WHAT? Now this Bumi guy is a little crazy, but he's an old friend of Aang's and I can't imagine anyone Aang trusts giving up his city so easily. But that's apparently what happened.

"It doesn't matter now," the resistance leader added. "Fighting the Fire Nation is the only path to freedom."

"Actually, there's another path to freedom," Aang replied. "You could leave Omashu."

The Earthbenders gave us another surprised look, but they were willing to hear us out. It was my job to come up with a plan, something that would make the Fire Nation WANT everyone to leave.

"You're all about to come down with a nasty case of pentapox."

🔴 🔴 🔴

Throughout the city, Earth Kingdom citizens put pentapi on their faces and arms causing red spots to appear. "The spots make you look sick, but you have to act sick too," I advised.

I gave them a few pointers, and then we were ready to put my brilliant plan into action. "Okay, everyone into the sick formation. Let's go!"

Wouldn't you know it, the Fire Nation governor

bought our scheme completely! He ordered all the "infected" people out of the city, but Aang stayed behind to find Bumi. I guess it doesn't matter what Bumi did to his city, Aang will stay loyal to his friend—even if he is insane!

I helped the others set up camp just outside the city. Aang returned a while later, with no news about Bumi. Then we discovered we had another problem. The little boy whose family we had saved earlier from the boulders had followed us out, and it turns out that it was the family of the Fire Nation governor!

The governor's son is cute, but he insisted on playing with my boomerang like it was a toy. "No. Bad Fire Nation baby!" I scolded.

I took it away from him and he started screaming. I gave in. "Oh, all right. Here."

Just then a messenger hawk flew into our camp with a scroll.

"It's from the governor," Aang said. "He thinks we took his son. He wants to make a trade—his son for King Bumi."

Even though this seemed too convenient to me, Aang, Katara, and I headed back into the city with the kid.

"You realize we're probably walking into a trap," I said.

"I don't think so," Aang said. Sometimes he can be a little too trusting.

When we arrived at the meeting place, we were surprised that the governor was not there. Instead there were three girls, including one I recognized as the governor's daughter—the one with the flying daggers. I'd better keep my eyes wide open and my boomerang ready.

They lowered Bumi down on a chain. He was stuck in a metal container—totally Earthbending-proof. Then the governor's daughter stepped forward.

"The deal's off," she announced. Uh, did I miss something? What happened?

As Bumi's box rose up, the governor's daughter began flinging her daggers. I was right. This was a trap!

"We've got to get the baby out of here!" Katara cried.

"Way ahead of you!" I replied, dashing away with the kid.

Signaling for Appa to get us out, I blew on Aang's bison whistle when someone tripped me.

I skidded toward the edge of the high platform, but managed to stop before we fell off.

Then, hopping onto Appa's back, I flew around to help Katara just as one of the girls— Ty Lee—pinched her, cutting off her chi and her ability to bend.

The governor's daughter, whose name was Mai, pulled out a three-prong dagger. "How are you going to fight without your bending?" she taunted Katara.

I could not believe she said that. Like only benders can fight. Obviously she'd never met ME before. I flung my boomerang at the girl, knocking the dagger from her hand. "I seem to manage," I said.

I helped Katara onto Appa and we flew to get Aang, who had been fighting off the third girl and trying to rescue Bumi. He didn't get Bumi, but at least he got rid of the girl.

Aang returned the little guy to his parents. I'm going to miss the kid. Well, except for the whole boomerang—touching thing.

Chapter 3

As we flew over the Earth Kingdom I glanced down and saw that we were right above a thick, swampy forest. Suddenly a huge tornado came out of nowhere!

"Faster! We've got to go faster!" I called, but it was no use. We were going down!

The tornado tossed us around and around and we finally splashed down into the swamp. Katara and Aang landed next to me, but there were no signs of Appa or Momo. They could be anywhere in the thick tangle of vines, roots, and branches. Fortunately, I had the right tool for dealing with unruly forests—a machete.

"Maybe we should be a little nicer to the swamp," Aang said as I started hacking away.

"Aang, these are just plants," I said, not bothering to stop.

That night we made camp and quickly dozed off. But before I could fall into deep sleep, something woke me up. It was a vine! It had a tight hold of my ankle and was pulling me deeper into the jungle. I had to slice my way free and run, but wouldn't you know it, the vines started chasing me!

The swamp was alive. "I'm sorry, swamp, I'm sorry, but please don't drag me into the murky water," I said. Then it let go of me.

"Stupid swamp," I muttered. I had to find the others to tell them what happened, but I stumbled and plopped down into the muck. Then I heard someone calling my name. "Hello? Is there anyone there?" I called back.

I looked up toward the voice and couldn't believe my eyes. A ghostly image floated above the swamp. It was Yue, princess of the Northern Water Tribe. A girl I really cared about. And who I couldn't save at the North Pole. No, it couldn't be her. That's impossible. Yue was gone—forever.

This was just a trick of the light, or swamp gas. I rubbed my eyes and took a deep breath—and Yue was still there.

"You didn't protect me," she said, and disappeared. I felt even more sad and alone. I miss you, Yue. I'm sorry I let you down.

I continued wandering through the stupid swamp for what seemed like forever. Then I heard a noise. Something was coming toward me. I tightened my grip on the machete, and— OOF! Whatever it was just crashed into me.

"Aang! Katara! What are you doing? I've been looking all over for you!" I exclaimed, excited to see them.

"I was chasing some girl," Aang said.

"I thought I saw Mom," Katara added.

"Look we were all just scared and hungry and our minds were playing tricks on us," I told them. "That's why we all saw things."

"All our visions led us here," Aang said, a little too knowingly.

"Okay, so where is 'here'?"

"It's the heart of the swamp. It's been calling to us."

Okay, this was some of that creepy,

magical Avatar stuff that I have a hard time buying. If I can't see something, eat something, or battle something, I don't believe in it.

Suddenly a huge swamp monster rose up from the water and attacked us! After a long battle, with me slashing and Aang and Katara bending, we discovered that it was just a Waterbender bending the water in the vines.

"See? Completely reasonable," I said to Aang. "Not a monster. Just a guy defending his home."

"This whole swamp is actually just one tree, spread out over miles," the Waterbender explained. "The tree is one big living organism. Just like the entire world."

Oh, great. More magical, mystical Avatar stuff. But when Aang touched the huge tree, he had a vision of Appa and Momo. He saw where they were.

We wasted no time in rescuing them from some local Waterbenders and finally got out of the swamp. If I never see another one again it'll be too soon!

We arrived in the Earth Kingdom town of Gaoling. A guy on the street handed us a flyer for Master Yu's Earthbending Academy, and it had a coupon good for one free Earthbending lesson.

"Maybe this could be the Earthbending teacher you're looking for," Katara said to Aang.

But the guy at the academy turned out to be a sleazebag. All he was interested in was getting Aang's money. Then we heard about an Earthbending tournament, called Earth Rumble Six, where the best Earthbenders in the world would be competing.

It was kind of a win—win thing. Aang would get to see the best Earthbenders, hoping that one of them might be able to teach him, and I would get to be in the crowd for the sporting event of the year.

After a few preliminary matches, the champion came out—and it was a young girl who was blind! She called herself the Blind Bandit. How in the world did she become the champ?

"She can't really be blind," Katara said. "It's just part of her character, right?"

"I think she is," Aang said.

"I think she's going down!" I said.

But no, she fought hard, Earthbending like crazy and beating a guy called the Boulder, who was three times her size. It was amazing!

After that defeat, the guy who ran the tournament, Xin Fu, made an announcement. "I'm offering this sack of gold to anyone who can defeat the Blind Bandit!" There was silence. "What? No one dares to face her?" he taunted the crowd.

All of a sudden Aang jumped into the ring. "I will!" he shouted.

"Go, Aang! Avenge the Boulder!" If anyone could beat the Blind Bandit, it would be Aang. He was going to wipe her out!

But then Aang said the weirdest thing to the Blind Bandit. "I don't want to fight you. I want to talk to you," he said.

Okay, Aang, you have lost your mind. No talking! We're here to win! Well, the Blind Bandit didn't want to talk, anyway. She just wanted to fight. So they finally fought, and Aang beat her. All right, Aang! As his manager, I jumped into the ring and snatched up the sack of gold.

"Way to go, champ!" I exclaimed loudly.

Later, Aang told me that he thought the Blind Bandit was the Earthbending teacher he had been looking for.

"She was the girl in my vision in the swamp," he explained.

Apparently when Aang was trying to rescue Bumi, the former Earth King had told him to find an Earthbending teacher who waited and listened. "That's what the Blind Bandit did to beat all those other guys," Aang added excitedly. "We've got to find her!"

So we tracked the girl to this amazing "rich people" estate. You know, huge house, sprawling gardens. We're talking big bucks. Some family called the Beifongs. We snuck onto the grounds and surprised the girl, the Blind Bandit.

I guess she wasn't too happy about it because the next moment the ground shot up under my feet. How in the world did she do that?

"What are you doing here?" the girl demanded.

"Well, a crazy king told me I had to find an Earthbender who listens to the earth," Aang explained. "Then I had a vision in a magic swamp and—"

Katara took over. "What Aang is trying to say is that he's the Avatar, and if he doesn't master Earthbending soon he won't be able to defeat the Fire Lord."

"Not my problem," the Blind Bandit said. "Now get out of here or I'll call the guards."

She didn't realize how wrong she was! It's obvious people like her are going to wait until the Fire Nation breaks down their doors before they realize that this war affects all of us. "Look, we all have to do our part to win this war, and yours is teaching Aang Earthbending," I insisted.

"Guards!" she screamed.

We immediately scrambled back over the wall. Okay, time to come up with a way to convince her that we are not crazy, that we have a truly important mission.

Aang came up with a plan. I know, that's usually my job, but occasionally I like to let other people share in a bit of glory. We went right up to the front door and announced that the Avatar was here to see the very important Beifong family. It worked! We were invited in for dinner. Not bad, Aang.

Sometimes being with the Avatar has its perks.

The Blind Bandit, whose real name is Toph, was not pleased to see us. Especially when Aang tried his best to convince her why she had to be his teacher. And then, get this, we find out that Toph's parents have no idea she's the Blind Bandit! They don't know that she's a great Earthbender. They think she's a helpless little blind girl!

We were completely taken aback. Every time Aang tried to point out how good she is, she kicked him with an Earthbending shot under the table. Weird.

Later that night Toph came to our room. Aang thought she wanted to fight.

"Relax," she said. "Look, I'm sorry about dinner. Let's call a truce, okay?"

"What's the catch?" Aang asked suspiciously.

"I just want to talk." The two of them headed outside.

Fine by me. I settled down in my cushy bed for a good night's sleep.

But not for long. Someone burst into the room to tell Katara and me that Aang and

Toph had been captured. We rushed outside, where I found a piece of paper.

"Whoever took Aang and Toph left this," I said.

"A ransom note!" Katara said. "It says, 'If you want to see your daughter again bring five hundred gold pieces to the arena.' It's signed by Xin Fu and the Boulder."

Hurrying back to the Earthbending arena with Toph's father, we found Aang and Toph trapped in cages! They were surrounded by Xin Fu and a bunch of Earthbenders.

"Here's your money," I said furiously, tossing the sack of gold to the ground. "Now let them go."

Xin Fu let Toph go, but he decided to keep Aang. "The Fire Nation will pay a hefty price for the Avatar. Now get out of my ring."

I was not about to let him get away with that. Still, I didn't know if Katara and I could take all these Earthbenders by ourselves. We needed Toph, but she was standing with her dad. What was she going to do? Would she let them take Aang to protect her precious little secret, or would she help us with some white—

hot Earthbending moves?

"Toph, we need you," Katara pleaded.

"My daughter is blind and helpless," said Toph's father. "She cannot help you."

"Yes, I can!" Toph said. And boy, did she help. All right . . . she did it all herself.

Toph put on an amazing demonstration of Earthbending. She knocked all the other Earthbenders, including Xin Fu himself, right out of the ring.

I still don't know how she does all that without seeing.

After we freed Aang, he explained that Toph sees using Earthbending. She uses her feet to feel the vibrations caused by any movement. I was impressed.

Now things should be great for Toph because her father knows what an awesome Earthbender she really is. But instead of being proud of her, he was angry!

"I've let you have far too much freedom," Toph's father told her when we were back at his house. "From now on you will be cared for and guarded twenty-four hours a day!"

What was his problem? He has a daughter

who's an amazing Earthbender, and he just wants to keep her locked up? I don't get it. He should want to show off her gift.

"Toph needs freedom to see the world and experience new things," Aang said.

Toph's father didn't even bother responding to Aang. He told his guards sternly, "Please escort the Avatar and his friends out. They are no longer welcome here."

I couldn't believe he was kicking us out! Oh, well. Good—bye, cushy bed.

"I'm sorry, Toph," Aang said.

"Good—bye, Aang," she replied sadly.

But a short while later, as we were preparing to leave on Appa, Toph came running up to us.

"My dad changed his mind," she said. "He said I was free to see the world."

Mr. Beifong didn't seem like the kind of guy who would change his mind so quickly, but I wasn't about to ask any questions. I was glad she was coming with us. Now Aang could learn Earthbending.

"We'd better leave before your dad changes his mind again," I said.

Chapter 4

It was late afternoon when we landed in a small clearing in a wooded area. We began unloading our supplies to set up camp.

"Hey, you guys picked a great campsite," Toph said. "The grass is so soft."

"That's not grass," I pointed out. "Appa's shedding." His fur was all over the place.

That night Toph suddenly rushed out of her tent. "There's something coming toward us!"

We couldn't see anything, but we trusted Toph. We packed up all our stuff and climbed onto Appa's back before flying away just in time.

Sure enough, from above, we spotted a strange—looking metal tank chugging beneath us. We found another clearing and landed. And once again we unloaded our supplies and set up camp.

All this work, and I was so tired. Then Katara and Toph started arguing. Toph didn't want to unload or set up camp.

"Ever since you joined us you've been nothing but selfish and unhelpful!" Katara shouted.

"What?" Toph screamed. "Look here, sugar queen, I gave up everything to teach Aang Earthbending, so don't talk to me about being selfish."

"Sugar queen?" Katara repeated, shocked at what Toph had called her.

I laughed. Sugar queen. I have to give Toph credit for that one!

"Should we do something?" Aang asked me, a little concerned.

"Hey, I'm just enjoying the show," I said. It's better not to get involved with two angry girls.

But the arguing continued. "Hey, how's a guy supposed to sleep with all this yelling and earthquaking?" I said.

And wouldn't you know it, that tank thing came back, so we had to pack up and leave AGAIN. I didn't know when I would get to sleep—if ever!

Our next campsite was on the side of a tall mountain. Now I was officially exhausted. The bags under my eyes had bags. I had no plans to set up camp. All I wanted to do was stretch out on the softest pile of dirt I could find and go to sleep. I thought I could finally relax without worrying about that tank following us.

Then Toph jumped up.

"Oh, no! Don't tell me," I whined.

"Let's get out of here," Katara said, but Aang had a different plan this time.

"Maybe we should face them," he said. "Who knows, maybe they're friendly."

I sighed. "You're always the optimist, Aang." Nobody would go to all that trouble in a big scary-looking machine just to say, "Hi, how ya doing? Why don't we be friends?"

And a couple of minutes later I was proven right. The tank appeared and from its belly came those three crazy girls who fought us in Omashu, charging toward us on their mongoose-dragons.

It was clear they weren't coming to bring us a housewarming gift for our new campsite!

"We can take them," Toph announced, setting herself in a battle stance. "Three on three!"

Uh, I know she's blind and everything, but . . . I had to correct her. "Actually Toph, there's four of us."

"Oh, sorry," she said, not sounding sorry at all. "I didn't count you. You know, no bending and all."

And I was actually starting to like having her around! "I can still fight!" I snapped.

"Okay," she relented. "Three on three— plus Sokka."

Now I understood why Katara was arguing with her all the time! She knows how to make people mad.

The crazy girls continued to charge toward us. Toph created a wall of rock to stop them, but that didn't pose a problem. The Firebending girl just blasted the rock away and kept on coming. I have to say that she was one scary–looking Firebender! I had seen enough—I didn't need a closer look.

"Let's get out of here!" I yelled.

We got back on Appa and returned to the sky.

"I can't believe those girls followed us all the way from Omashu!" Katara said. "The crazy blue Firebending and the flying daggers are bad enough, but the last time we saw them, one of those girls did something that took my bending away. That's scary!"

I was exhausted. We were all exhausted, even Appa. And then, as if to prove the point, Appa fell asleep in midair, and we started to plunge toward the ground. We screamed. This was not the time to fall asleep!

"Appa's exhausted," Aang said. "We have to land." And so we set down near a river.

"Okay, we've put a lot of distance between us and them," I said when we landed. "The plan right now is to get some sleep!"

That's when Katara and Toph started up again. "Of course we could've gotten some sleep earlier if Toph didn't have such issues about helping," Katara said.

"What?" Toph cried. "You're blaming ME for this? If there's anyone to blame, it's Sheddy over there."

She pointed at Appa. "You want to know how they keep finding us? He's leaving a trail of fur everywhere we go!"

"How dare you blame Appa!" Aang shouted. "He saved your life three times today!"

Okay . . . I see there's not going to be any sleep for me anytime soon.

"Appa never had a problem flying when it was just the three us," Aang added harshly.

And all of a sudden it got really quiet. No one said anything and no one did anything— until Toph picked up her bags. "See ya," she said, as she headed toward the woods.

This was not good. We needed her. Aang needed her. I had to stop her.

"Wait!" I called out. But Toph pushed me away as she disappeared into the forest. I shot a look at Aang and Katara.

Nice going, guys. You blew off your Earthbending teacher and our early warning system for those psycho girls following us in their nasty tank.

"What did I just do?" Aang cried. "I yelled at my Earthbending teacher . . . and now she's gone."

"I was so mean to her," Katara added.

"Yeah, you two were pretty much jerks," I said.

"We need to find Toph and apologize," Katara said. I agreed, but I also had a question: "What are we going to do about the tank full of dangerous ladies chasing us?"

Aang came up with a plan. "You guys take Momo and Appa and go find Toph," he said. "I'm going to use some of Appa's fur to make a fake trail and lead the tank off course."

It was a good idea, but the crazy girls figured out the plan. Plus, Appa was just too tired to fly fast enough or high enough to avoid being spotted. So we soon saw two of the girls riding their mongoose-dragons, hot on our trail.

The girl from Omashu started throwing her flying daggers at me, but I was able to defend myself with my boomerang and club. Katara faced off with the girl who had blocked her chi before. We both fought hard, but in the end, it was Appa who saved us with an awesome Airbending move. Then we got out of there quick!

We caught up with Aang in a deserted town. He was being attacked by the Firebending girl. Zuko and his uncle were there too. We quickly landed and joined the battle.

Then, just when the Firebending girl was about to unleash one of her powerful blue lightning attacks, Toph showed up and knocked her to the ground with an Earthbending move.

"I thought you guys could use a little help," Toph said. I don't know what made her change her mind, but I was so happy she came back. We all surrounded the Firebender, who turned out to be Zuko's sister, Princess Azula! Great.

"Well, look at this," Azula cackled. "Enemies and traitors all working together. I'm done. I know when I'm beaten. A princess surrenders with honor."

It looked like she was going to surrender. She bowed her head, then all of a sudden, she blasted her uncle! This prompted everyone to immediately unleash attacks at her. But when the smoke cleared, she was gone.

Zuko ran to his uncle's side. The man was badly hurt, but it looked like he was going to make it.

"Zuko, I can help," Katara said, ready to use her healing ability.

"Get away from me!" Zuko shouted, before unleashing a fire blast just above our heads. "Leave!"

He didn't have to tell us twice. I was ready to go. And there was only one way to end this crazy long day. Appa flew us to a mountain ledge where we all stretched out and finally fell into a wonderful, deep sleep.

Chapter 5

After many days of traveling, we stopped for a rest on an open prairie.

Everyone felt like we needed a break. Aang had been training hard, practicing both Earthbending and Waterbending. So everyone chose a vacation spot. Everyone except me, that is.

"There's no time for vacations, Aang," I said. "Even if you do master all of the elements, then what? It's not like we have a map of the Fire Nation. We need information. We need intelligence. And we're not going to get that taking vacations."

I was voted down, of course. What a shock. I was the only one who wasn't either teaching or learning. Mr. Not–A–Bender here.

Next, for Katara's vacation, we traveled to some place called Misty Palms Oasis.

Well, the "oasis" was actually a dump— a rundown cantina with some lowlife Sandbenders hanging around like annoying bugs. Good choice, Katara. This was way more important than planning our strategy against the Fire Nation.

But it was in that flea trap that we met Professor Zei, an anthropologist and professor from Ba Sing Se University. He was searching for a lost library run by some spirit called Wan Shi Tong. The place was supposed to have books from all over the world, which meant that they might have some useful information or maps of the Fire Nation.

"For my vacation, I choose finding that library," I said eagerly.

Off we went, flying on Appa, with the professor guiding the way. We flew over the desert, which was one vast sea of brown. There was nothing but sand for miles. . . . Then I spotted something sticking out of the sand. "Down there. What's that?"

We landed and found a tower jutting out from the sand. I looked at Professor Zei's picture of the enormous library and realized that the thing we were looking at was the top spire of the building! "This is the library," I announced. "But it's completely buried in the sand!"

Toph used Earthbending to determine that the inside of the library was still completely intact, then we climbed up the spire and slipped in through a window. We left Toph to wait outside with Appa.

The place was huge! I had a really good feeling that we were going to find what we needed on the Fire Nation.

And then an enormous owl showed up.

"Are you the spirit who brought this library into the physical world?" I asked.

"Indeed. I am Wan Shi Tong, and you are obviously humans, who, by the way, are no longer permitted in the library."

"What do you have against humans?" Aang asked.

"Humans only bother learning things to get the edge on other humans. So who are you trying to destroy?"

Uh . . . how did he know? Was it written on our faces? I had to fake him out. "No, no destroying. We have come here to seek knowledge for knowledge's sake." Yes, that's a pretty good answer.

But the owl wasn't so easily fooled. "If you are going to lie to an all-knowing spirit being, you should at least put a little effort into it," he said.

I had to cover fast. "I'm not lying," I said. "I'm here with the Avatar, and he's the bridge between our worlds. He'll vouch for me."

"We will not abuse your library, good spirit. You have my word," Aang assured him.

I held my breath as we all waited for his response.

"Very well," the spirit said.

Whew! Now we just had to find something that would help us defeat the Fire Nation.

What I found was even more than I could have hoped for. First I discovered a burned scrap of paper with a date and the words "The Darkest Day in Fire Nation History." Then one of the owl's assistants, a fox, led us to a mechanical planetarium that showed the position of the sun, moon, and stars on any given day. Using this amazing machine we figured out that the date on the paper was the date of a solar eclipse—a day when the moon blocks out the sun. And during a solar eclipse, Firebenders lose their bending abilities.

This was it! This was the way to beat the Fire Nation!

"We just have to figure out when the next solar eclipse is happening," I told the others. "Then we've got to get that information to Ba Sing Se so the Earth King can plan to invade the Fire Nation on that day. The Fire Lord is going down!"

Just then there was an uncomfortable silence and I felt someone behind me. When I spun around, I saw the owl towering over us.

"Mortals are so predictable," the owl said. "And such terrible liars. You betrayed my trust."

"We're just trying to protect the people we love," I replied.

"And I'm going to protect what I love. I'm taking my knowledge back. No one will ever abuse it again."

The owl began flapping his wings and the

library started sinking into the desert.

Oh, no! He's destroying the library. And he's going to take us along with it!

We ran from the planetarium. But then I realized that we needed one more important piece of information: the date of the next eclipse.

"Sokka, let's go!" Katara called.

"If we leave this place we'll never get the information we need," I said. "Aang, come with me!"

While Katara and Momo tried to distract the owl, Aang and I hurried back to the planetarium. There we checked every day between now and the time that Sozin's Comet—the comet that will give the Fire Nation unlimited power—returns. In a few minutes we had the date. "That's it! The solar eclipse. It's just a few months away. Now let's get this info to Ba Sing Se!"

Aang and I met up with Katara and Professor Zei, who decided to stay and sink with the library. I think he's crazy for wanting to stay, but I guess he really loves to read. We, on the other hand, had to get out. Aang flew us back up the spire and out the window.

Toph had been holding up the building with

Earthbending! Once she saw that we were safe, she let it go and the entire library disappeared into the sand.

"We did it!" I yelled. "We got the information we need to stop the Fire Nation, and . . . where's Appa?"

That's when Toph told us that he was missing. Gone. Taken by a group of Sandbenders. And here we were in the middle of a desert, with no way out.

Big deal that we had the information that could stop the Fire Nation. What good would it do us if we never made it out of the desert?

Aang was furious. "How could you let them take Appa?" he shouted at Toph. "Why didn't you stop them?"

"I couldn't," she replied. "The library was sinking and you guys were still inside."

"I'm going after Appa," Aang declared, before taking off on his glider.

"Well, we'd better start walking," Katara suggested.

Why? What good would that do? We couldn't walk all the way to Ba Sing Se. We were doomed. There was no other way to look at it.

We walked on under the blazing sun. We got thirsty, but we had very little water. I found a cactus plant and drank some of its juice. Everything got a little fuzzy after that, and I really don't remember much about our journey across the desert. All I know is that we had to figure out a way to get to Ba Sing Se, and we had to try to find Appa.

After a while Aang returned without finding Appa. But we did find a sandsailing boardlike thing that Aang powered with Airbending. It was nice to know that we didn't have to walk all the way to Ba Sing Se.

As my head cleared we were attacked by a flock of flying buzzard—wasps. Nasty creatures. Luckily a group of Sandbenders came to our rescue, but then they wanted to know why we had a Sandbender sailer.

"Our bison was stolen," Katara explained. "We found this sailer in the desert."

"You dare accuse our people of theft when you ride on a stolen sandsailer!" one of the Sandbenders shouted.

"I recognize that voice," Toph whispered. "He's the Sandbender who took Appa."

"You stole Appa!" Aang screamed. "Where is he?"

And then Aang lost it. He blasted the Sandbenders' sand ships. That made the Sandbender confess.

"I didn't know he belonged to the Avatar," the frightened Sandbender said. "I traded him to some nomads. He's probably in Ba Sing Se by now. They were going to sell him there."

At that moment Aang went into the Avatar state. A huge wind funnel spun all around him. We had to get out of the way! I grabbed Toph and helped her run clear of the funnel. I looked around for Katara. Oh, no, what was she doing?

My sister actually walked toward Aang, right into the heart of the tornado that he had spun. Somehow she made it in and reached him. She hugged him, and slowly the winds died down.

Sometimes my sister is pretty amazing. But don't tell her I said that.

Chapter 6

We needed to get to Ba Sing Se as quickly as possible to deliver our information. We left the desert and arrived at an area filled with lakes and waterfalls. According to the map I took from the library in the desert, there was only one way to get to the city.

"It looks like the only passage through all this water is a sliver of land called Serpent's Pass," I said.

Then a family of refugees showed up. They were also going to Ba Sing Se.

"Great," said Katara. "We can travel together through Serpent's Pass."

"Serpent's Pass?" one of the refugees said. "Only the truly desperate take that deadly route!"

"Deadly route," said Toph. "Great pick, Sokka."

Well, it didn't say "deadly route" on the map! We headed for the ferry instead.

🔄 🔄 🔄

At the ferry dock I felt a hand grab my collar. I turned to see a female security officer staring right at me.

"Is there a problem?" I asked, slightly annoyed.

"Yeah, I've got a problem with you," the guard said. "I've seen your type before. Sarcastic, think you're hilarious. And let me guess. You're traveling with the Avatar."

Whoa—who was this person? How did she know this about me? "Do I know you?" I asked suspiciously.

Then, of all things, she leaned in and kissed me! That's when I knew.

"Suki!" I yelled out.

"Hey, Sokka. It's so good to see you."

It was incredible to see Suki again. She is a Kyoshi warrior we met during our travels. And I really like her—a lot! It turned that out she had been working at the ferry helping refugees.

Just then someone stole the passports and tickets of the family of refugees we were traveling with, which meant they couldn't take the ferry.

"Don't worry," Aang said. "I'll lead you through Serpent's Pass."

Aw, Aang. Did we really have to do that? We gave up our tickets on the nice safe ferry to go on the deadly route for desperate people.

"I'm coming too," Suki said.

"Are you sure that's a good idea?" I asked, suddenly afraid that something might happen to her. It could be dangerous. She would probably be safer staying at the ferry dock.

"Sokka, I thought you'd want me to come," she said softly.

"I do. It's just—"

"Just what?"

"Nothing. I'm glad you're coming," I said with a smile. This trip just got a whole lot more complicated.

🪙 🪙 🪙

We arrived at the pass, which was a thin strip of land between two lakes—and were immediately attacked by Fire Nation ships patrolling the lake!

They lobbed a volley of fireballs at us. One of the fireballs hit the cliff above us and started a rockslide that headed right for Suki!

Dashing forward I pushed Suki out of the way. She fell clear of the tumbling rocks that somehow missed me, too.

"Suki! Are you okay? You have to be more careful!" I scolded. When I think that I could have lost her forever right then and there . . .

That night we set up camp, and I couldn't help worrying about Suki. She was putting her stuff really close to the edge! What was she thinking? "You shouldn't sleep there," I said. "Who knows how stable this ledge is. It could give way at any moment."

"Sokka, I'm fine," she replied.

"You're right, you're right," I said. "You're perfectly capable of taking care of yourself." Maybe I was being overprotective. After all, she is a Kyoshi warrior.

"Wait!" I called out. Was that a spider crawling on her sleeping bag? Was it poisonous? What if it bit her in the middle of the night?

"Oh, never mind. I thought I saw a spider . . . but you're fine."

Suki didn't have anything to say, so I went to set up my own stuff and go to sleep. Except that I couldn't. There was too much to worry about. So I decided to take a walk, instead.

Apparently Suki couldn't sleep either—she was walking around, too.

"Look, I know you're just trying to help, but I can take care of myself," she told me.

"I know you can," I replied.

"Then why are you acting so overprotective?"

How could I explain this to her? Should I tell her about losing Yue?

"It's so hard to lose someone you care about," I said. "Something happened at the North Pole, and I couldn't protect someone. I don't ever want anything like that to happen again."

I have never stopped thinking about Princess Yue. I don't want to lose Suki like that.

And then Suki said something that threw me off guard. "I lost someone I cared about, too. He didn't die, he just went away. He was smart and brave and funny."

Well, how can I compete with a guy like that? "Who is this guy? Is he taller than me? Is he better looking?"

"It is YOU, stupid!" Suki said.

"Oh . . . ," I said, suddenly feeling really dumb. I guess I missed the point completely. Suki really cares about me! We looked into each other's eyes for a long moment. I feel so much for Suki—and yet I'm not sure how I should feel. Argh! Why do I have to think so much?

Then Suki leaned in to kiss me! What more could I want? Suki is great, and she thinks I'm smart and brave and funny. It's . . . it's . . . I couldn't. I had to back away.

"I'm sorry," Suki said, embarrassed.

"No, you shouldn't be," I replied, getting up and walking away instead of telling her why she didn't need to feel bad.

It's not you, Suki. It's me. I can't risk caring for somebody again. Not like I cared for Yue. It hurts too much when you lose them. It's not a chance I'm willing to take. I'm sorry, Suki. I'm really sorry.

The next day I found out why they call the route Serpent's Pass. A real-life giant sea serpent attacked!

As Aang and Katara battled the creature, Toph tumbled into the lake.

"Help! I can't swim!" she cried out. Then she vanished into the water.

"I'm coming, Toph!" I called out. I had to save her. I started to pull off my boots, and then—hey, Suki just dove right in with all her clothes on. She's a good swimmer, and she had no problem rescuing Toph. They're both okay. Whew! That's a relief. I would have saved Toph. I just wanted to get my boots off first.

Meanwhile, Aang and Katara finished off the sea serpent. (Good thing we have them around!) A short while later we came to the end of Serpent's Pass.

Aang took off to find Appa. "See you in the big city," he said.

Then Suki came up to me. "Sokka, it's been really great to see you again."

"Why does it sound like you're saying good-bye?" I asked.

"I came along to make sure you got through Serpent's Pass safely," she replied. "But now I have to get back to the other Kyoshi warriors."

What a dope I am. She was there to protect ME all along. No wonder she couldn't stand me acting so protective.

Then she started to apologize, "Listen, Sokka, I'm sorry about last night, I—"

Kiss her, Sokka. Just kiss her. "You talk too much," I said, before kissing her.

🏵 🏵 🏵

When we reached the outer wall of Ba Sing Se we were surprised to see Aang land beside us.

"What are you doing here?" Katara asked. "I thought you were looking for Appa."

"I was," said Aang. "But something stopped me. Something big."

Aang took us to the top of the outer wall, where we could see a huge scary–looking drill coming toward us. The Fire Nation was about to invade the city of Ba Sing Se!

We had to find a way to stop the invasion. Our first stop was the infirmary to visit some Earthbenders who had already gotten injured trying to stop the drill.

Katara examined an Earthbending captain. "His chi is blocked," she said. Then she asked him, "Who did this to you?"

"Two girls ambushed us," the captain replied. "One hit me with some quick jabs and suddenly I couldn't Earthbend anymore."

"Ty Lee!" Katara exclaimed. "She doesn't look dangerous, but she knows the human body and its weak points. It's like she takes you down from the inside."

And that's when I got my most brilliant idea yet. I knew how we could defeat that drill—by taking it down from inside.

🔅 🔅 🔅

We snuck onto the drill, and Aang and Katara started cutting away at its support braces with a whiplike Waterbending move.

Somehow I had envisioned it going a little faster, and as the two slowly made small cuts in the braces, I realized we would never cut through all of them in time. I had to figure out what more I could do.

But it was Aang who came up with an idea. "Maybe we don't need to cut all the way through each brace. If we weaken them all, I can deliver one big blow from above . . ."

Aha! I got it! "And BOOM! It all comes crashing down."

Aang and Katara started on Plan B, working quickly to make cuts in a series of braces. Just as they slashed the final brace,

Azula, Mai, and Ty Lee showed up.

"Guys, get out of here!" Aang shouted to us. "I know what I need to do!"

I heard Aang's command, but Ty Lee gave me a LOOK. I think she likes me. And I have to admit, she is cute. I mean, I know she's Fire Nation and all, but—

"Sokka!"

"Okay, Katara. I'm coming!" I yelled back. Sisters can be so annoying.

Katara and I climbed into a big pipe filled with slurry and rode the current, popping out at the end of the tunnel. I knew it was just rocks and water mixed together, but it was still disgusting. It was in my mouth, eyes, ears—everywhere!

A few seconds later Ty Lee came out of the pipe, and Katara used Waterbending to trap her in the sludge. Then Aang slammed the drill from above and the whole thing collapsed.

We did it! We destroyed the Fire Nation drill!

"I just want to say, good effort out there today, Team Avatar," I told the others. Team Avatar. I like the sound of that. Now we're ready to head into Ba Sing Se!

Chapter 7

We took the train from the outer wall into the city itself. There we were met by a woman who somehow knew who we were.

"Hello, my name is Joo Dee," she said. "I have been given the great honor of showing the Avatar around Ba Sing Se. And you must be Sokka, Katara, and Toph. Shall we get started?"

This was great. She'd know where the Earth King was. This was going to be easier than I imagined. "Yes," I said. "We have information about the Fire Nation that we need to deliver to the Earth King immediately."

"Great! Let's begin our tour, then I'll show you to your new home."

I was confused. Maybe she hadn't heard what I said, so I tried again. "We need to talk to the king about the war. It's important."

"You're in Ba Sing Se now. Everyone is safe here."

What was this lady's problem? It's like she was totally ignoring me—not to mention ignoring reality. She didn't realize how wrong she was. If we don't stop the Fire Nation, NOBODY will be safe anywhere.

But Joo Dee simply led us to a carriage and started our tour of the city. I tried to tell her again and again how important it was for us to see the king, but she ignored me each time.

"Maybe she's deaf?" I wondered out loud.

"She hears you," Toph said. "She's just not listening."

"Why won't she talk about the war?" Katara asked.

"Whatever her deal is, I don't like this place," Aang said. "We just need to find Appa and get out of here."

We passed the king's palace and saw some scary-looking guards. Joo Dee said that they were agents of the Dai Li, who guard the city's traditions.

"Can we see the king now?" Aang blurted out.

Joo Dee just laughed. "Oh, no. One doesn't just pop in on the king."

Now this was getting frustrating.

Then the carriage stopped in front of a really nice house.

"Here we are! Your new home!" Joo Dee said cheerfully, just as a messenger arrived with a scroll. She took it and read it quickly. Then she announced, "Good news! Your request to see the king is being processed and you should get to see him in about a month."

"A month!" We were going to have to stay in that weird place for a whole month? That wasn't going to leave us much time to prepare our attack on the Fire Nation.

"If we're going to be here for a whole month, we should spend our time looking for Appa," Aang said.

We searched all over the city. Not only had no one seen Appa, but everyone seemed scared to talk to us. Even our next–door neighbor was terrified.

"You can't mention the war here," he said. "And whatever you do, stay away from the Dai Li!"

I couldn't believe how crazy it was. Clearly we were not going to get help from anyone. Not from Joo Dee, not from our neighbors, and apparently not from the Dai Li. We were going to have to do it on our own. Which meant we needed a plan to get in to see the Earth King. He's the only one who could straighten everything out.

Later Katara saw something in the news–paper that gave her an idea. "The king is having a party at the palace tonight for his pet bear. We can sneak in with the crowd."

So that night, Katara and Toph dressed up as fancy ladies and went in first. Aang and I snuck in as busboys.

Then trouble came walking up to us. It was Joo Dee. "What are you doing here?" she wanted to know. "You have to leave immediately or we'll all be in terrible trouble."

I'd had it with her. "Not until we see the king!"

"You don't understand. You must go!"

But I wasn't about to leave. No one was going to tell us what to do. While Aang provided a distraction, I went to search for the king. A short while later he entered the ballroom. Then, as Aang rushed over to greet him, I was grabbed by two Dai Li guards and taken to a room along with Katara and Toph. A few minutes later Aang showed up with this guy Long Feng, the head of the Dai Li.

Ah, finally, someone who could give me some answers. "Why won't you let us talk to the king? We have information that could defeat the Fire Nation!"

"The Earth King has no time to get involved with political squabbles and the day—to—day minutia of military activities," Long Feng said.

"But this could be the most important thing he's ever heard!" Aang explained.

"What's most important to the king is maintaining the cultural heritage of Ba Sing Se. It's my job to oversee the rest of the city's resources, including the military."

So Long Feng was the guy who's really in power. This explained a lot.

"So the king is just a figurehead," Katara said.

"He's your puppet!" Toph added.

If this was the guy who's in charge, then maybe we'd come to the right place after all.

"We've found out about a solar eclipse that will leave the Fire Nation defenseless. You could lead an invasion—"

"Enough!" He angrily cut me off. "I don't want to hear your ridiculous plan. It is the strict policy of Ba Sing Se that the war not be mentioned within our walls."

It was all beginning to make sense. This guy had a sweet deal with all the power, and he was keeping the truth from the people of the city—not to mention from the king. This was corruption, plain and simple, and it was as bad as the Fire Nation itself.

"You can't keep the truth from all these people!" Katara shouted.

"I'll tell them," Aang said. "I'll make sure everyone knows."

"Until now you've been treated as honored guests," Long Feng said sternly. "But from now on you will be watched by Dai Li Agents. If you mention the war to anyone, you'll be expelled from the city."

He paused, watching our expressions before adding, "I understand you've been looking for your bison. It would be a shame if you were not able to complete your quest."

He's threatening us! He was going to kick us out before we had a chance to find Appa—and maybe he also knew where Appa was.

"Now Joo Dee will show you home," Long Feng said curtly before leaving.

A woman we had never seen before stepped into the room. "Come with me, please."

"What happened to Joo Dee?" Katara asked.

"I'm Joo Dee," the woman replied without hesitation.

Could this place get any weirder?

⊕ ⊕ ⊕

With our attempt to see the Earth King foiled, we turned our attention back to finding Appa. We put posters of the big furry guy up all over town, hoping that someone might have seen him. Shortly after we returned home the doorbell rang. It was Joo Dee—the first Joo Dee.

"Hello, Aang and Katara and Sokka and Toph," she said, smiling.

Of course she's smiling. She's always smiling. "What happened to you? Did the Dai Li throw you in jail?"

"Of course not! I simply took a short vacation to Lake Laogai, out in the country. It was quite relaxing."

"Why are you here?" Aang asked suspiciously.

Joo Dee pulled out one of our posters. "You are absolutely forbidden by the rules of the city to put up posters."

Great. Another thing that we're not allowed to do. We couldn't see the Earth King. We couldn't talk about the war. We couldn't put up posters. What good was it being here?

Aang was furious. "We don't care about the rules, and we're not asking permission! We're finding Appa on our own, and you should just stay out of our way!" Then he slammed the door in Joo Dee's face.

I winced. "That may come back to bite us in the blubber."

"I don't care," Aang said. "From now on we

do whatever it takes to find Appa."

"Yeah!" Toph agreed. "Let's break some rules!"

⊕ ⊕ ⊕

We headed back out to put up more posters and decided to split up to cover more ground. I took Toph with me. But it wasn't long before we heard a commotion coming from Katara's direction.

"Katara, what is it?" I asked.

"Jet's back," Katara answered before our eyes locked on the figure that was partly frozen and pinned to the wall behind her.

Jet was a rebel we met during our travels. He had done some pretty bad stuff, and Katara didn't trust him at all.

"I'm here to help you find Appa," he insisted. "I swear I've changed. I was a troubled person, and I let my anger get out of control. But I don't even have the gang now. I've put that all behind me."

"You're lying!" Katara said. Then Toph walked up to the wall and put her hand on it.

"He's not lying," she said. "I can feel his breathing and heartbeat. When people lie, there's a physical reaction. He's telling the truth."

"I heard two guys talking about some furry creature they had," Jet explained. "I figured it must be Appa."

Aang got all excited. "I bet they have Appa here in the city!"

Then we found out that Jet had been brainwashed by the Dai Li at their secret headquarters!

"Maybe Appa is in the same place they took Jet," Aang said hopefully. But Jet could not remember the name of the place.

"All I know is that it was under the water," Jet said. "Like under a lake."

That sounded familiar. "Remember what Joo Dee said?" I said. "She said she went on vacation to Lake Laogai."

"That's it!" Jet cried. "Lake Laogai!"

At last we had a lead to where Appa was. Now all we had to do was go there and rescue him!

Chapter 8

Jet led us to the shores of Lake Laogai.

"So where are the secret headquarters?" I asked.

"Under the water, I think," Jet replied.

Toph felt around with her feet. "There's a tunnel right there near the shore." Using Earthbending, she opened the entrance and we slipped inside.

Beneath the lake we found a complex filled with hallways, rooms, and prison cells. We passed a group of women all being trained to be Joo Dee! It was definitely one of the creepiest things we had ever seen.

"I think Appa's in here," Jet said, when we came to one of the doors.

But when we stepped into the room, we didn't find Appa. Instead we found Long Feng and his Dai Li soldiers! Maybe Katara was right to be so wary of Jet. Maybe he did lead us all into a trap!

"By breaking into Dai Li headquarters you have made yourselves enemies of the state," Long Feng said.

Enemies of the state. I kind of liked the sound of that.

"Take them into custody!"

That didn't sound quite as good.

We battled the Dai Li, and Jet fought against them as hard as we did. There was no doubt that he was on our side.

"Long Feng is escaping!" Katara shouted.

Aang and Jet took off after him. Toph, Katara, and I stayed and finished off the Dai Li. When we caught up with the others, we found Aang kneeling over Jet, who was hurt. Long Feng was nowhere to be seen.

Katara tried healing Jet, but he ordered us to leave, insisting that he would be all right. We didn't want to leave him, but we had no choice.

We had to find Appa before it was too late.

We hurried to a large cell, hoping Appa would still be in there. But when we got there it was empty.

"Appa's gone!" Aang cried. "Long Feng beat us here!"

"If we keep moving maybe we can catch up with them!" I said.

Toph guided us through the maze of tunnels back up to the shore. There, Dai Li agents closed in on us from every side.

"We're trapped!" Katara shouted.

Then Momo suddenly got all excited and took off into the sky.

"What is it, Momo?" Aang asked.

I looked up and gasped. It was Appa!

We didn't know how he got free, but we didn't care. We were just glad to see him again.

That big furball wasted no time in helping us. He knocked down the Dai Li, then bit Long Feng in the leg and tossed him into the lake. Then we all climbed onto Appa's back and headed up into the sky.

It was just like old times.

We came to Ba Sing Se for two reasons—to find Appa and to tell the Earth King about the solar eclipse. It was more important than ever that we complete the second part of our mission. "Now's the time to tell the Earth King our plan. We're going to need his support if we want to invade the Fire Nation when the eclipse comes," I said.

"And now that we have Appa back, there's nothing to stop us from telling the Earth King the truth about the war and about Long Feng's conspiracy," Aang said.

We flew back to the city and battled our way into the king's palace, fighting royal Earthbending guards who were trying to keep us out.

It was very strange—we were really on the same side, but we had to fight the guards as if they were the enemies, just for the chance to meet face-to-face with the king. I hoped it was worth it.

When we finally did reach the Earth King's throne room we found Long Feng by his side, along with some Dai Li agents and some royal Earthbending guards.

"We need to talk with you!" Aang told the Earth King.

Immediately Long Feng jumped in. "He's lying! They're here to overthrow you."

Overthrow the king? Well, that's really dumb. Why in the world would two people from the Water Tribe, an Earth Kingdom citizen, and the Avatar want to overthrow the leader of the Earth Kingdom? "No, we're on your side. We're here to help," I said.

"You have to trust us!" Katara added.

"You invade my palace, lay waste to all my guards, break down my fancy door, and you expect me to trust you?" the king replied.

"He has a good point," Toph said.

It was only when the king learned that Aang was the Avatar that he agreed at least to listen.

"There's a war going on right now—for the past one hundred years, in fact!" Aang explained. "The Dai Li have kept it a secret from you. It's a conspiracy to control the city and to control you!"

The king was really skeptical, but was willing to let us prove the conspiracy theory to him, so we boarded a train for Lake Laogai. And get this, we found out that the king had never been outside the palace before. Never! No wonder Long Feng could keep him in the dark about what was really going on in the world.

"Underneath Lake Laogai is the Dai Li's secret headquarters," I explained. "You're about to see where all the brainwashing and conspiring took place."

But when we arrived, the headquarters was gone.

"Oh, don't tell me!" I cried.

Katara and Toph used bending to try to find the opening, but it wasn't there. "There's nothing down there anymore," Toph said.

"I SAID 'don't tell me.'"

"The Dai Li must have destroyed the evi—dence," Katara said.

"This was a waste of my time!" the king said.

We had to think of something else. We finally had the Earth King's attention, but now we had nothing to show him. Or did we? "What about the drill?" I asked.

"That's it!" Katara cried. "They'll never be able to cover that up in time!"

We flew back to the city, and were relieved to see that the huge drill was still there.

"What is that?" the king asked when he saw it.

"A giant drill made by the Fire Nation to break through your walls," I explained. Now he would have to believe there's a war.

"This is nothing more than a construction project," someone said.

We all spun around to see Long Feng. He was still trying to convince the king we were lying.

"Then why is there a Fire Nation insignia on your construction project?" Katara asked.

That's my little sister. Sometimes she gets it right on the money! The king had Long Feng arrested and hauled off to jail. Justice is sweet!

Now that the Earth King knew we were telling him the truth, we could finally deliver the information we had worked so hard to get to him. "A solar eclipse is coming. The sun will be entirely blocked by the moon, and the Firebenders will be helpless," I said.

"What are you suggesting, Sokka?" the king asked.

"That the day we need to invade the Fire

Nation is the Day of the Black Sun."

"That would require moving troops out of Ba Sing Se. We'd be completely vulnerable."

He didn't get it, and I understood why. This was all new to him, and thinking of his city as anything other than a totally impenetrable fortress was foreign to him. But I had to convince him that he had no other choice.

"You're already vulnerable," I said. "The Fire Nation won't stop until Ba Sing Se falls. You can either sit back and wait for that to happen, or take the offensive and give yourself a fighting chance."

The Earth King thought for a few minutes. I could see that this was the most difficult decision he had ever had to make. "Very well. You have my support," he finally said.

Woo-hoo! We did it! We really might win this war after all! And things might actually get back to normal in the world.

As we were celebrating, General How, the leader of the Council of Generals, came into the throne room with some amazing news. "We've searched Long Feng's office. We've found some things that I believe will interest everybody. Long Feng kept secret files on everyone in Ba Sing Se, including you kids."

He had a letter from Toph's mother saying that she was here in the city and that she wanted to see Toph. He had a scroll that had been attached to Appa's horn when the Dai Li captured him. It was from a guru at the Eastern Air Temple—some kind of spiritual expert, according to Aang—who could help him take the next step in his Avatar journey.

But the best news of all came in the form of an intelligence report that a Water Tribe fleet was located near Chameleon Bay!

"It's Dad!" I couldn't believe it. Every day since we started our journey I've thought about seeing Dad again. Everything I do to help Aang, to help people fight the Fire Nation, I do to prove that I'm a warrior worthy of Dad's respect. And now, when things were finally looking up, we knew where he was. I had to go see him.

But then I remembered that someone needed to help the Earth King plan his invasion. I couldn't leave. Dad would have to wait.

Then Katara said something incredible. "No, Sokka," she said. "I know how badly you want to

85

help Dad. You go. I'll stay here with the king."

She is the best sister ever! She was giving up the chance to see Dad so that I could fight by his side. I remember crying on the day he left for the war because he wouldn't take me with him. I've always believed that he thought I wasn't ready. Well, there's no more crying. I was finally a man, a true warrior of the Water Tribe. And soon I'd be fighting at his side. I couldn't remember when I'd felt happier!

As we all prepared to go our separate ways, news came that the Kyoshi Warriors were in the city.

"That means Suki's here!" I said. "I don't have time to see her now, but that sure gives me something to look forward to when I get back." After a long group hug, we said our good-byes.

Aang and I took off on Appa. He was going to drop me off at Chameleon Bay on his way to the Eastern Air Temple. As the city faded from view I couldn't help but smile at how things were finally looking up for us. The Earth King was on our side, Long Feng was in jail, and Suki would be waiting for me when I returned.

And best of all, I was going to see Dad!

降
击
神
通

Chapter 9

Appa landed on a hill overlooking Chameleon Bay. I climbed down, glanced at the Water Tribe encampment below, and immediately felt nauseated. I didn't think I'd be so nervous seeing Dad again.

"You haven't seen your dad in more than two years," Aang said as he got ready to leave. "You must be so excited!"

"I know I should be, but I just feel sick to my stomach."

"Don't be nervous. He's going to be so happy to see you."

I nodded, even though in my heart I wasn't

sure. I watched as Aang flew away. "See you in a week!" he said. Then I was alone. I took a deep breath and started down the hill toward the camp.

I entered the camp and passed by some Water Tribe warriors.

I felt a little uncomfortable—they were staring at me like I didn't belong. . . . No, that wasn't it—they're staring at me because they recognized who I was. Then they came over to shake my hand!

Wow. I never expected a greeting like that! Maybe they heard about what I had been doing, or maybe it was just because of who my father is, but it sure felt good to be welcomed. One warrior pointed to a tent up ahead. Dad must be in there. If only he's as glad to see me as they were . . . well, here goes.

I stuck my head into the tent. Dad was there with his best friend, Bato, looking over a battle map. When Dad turned to look at me, his hard gaze met mine and I once again felt the power of his presence. Then his tough warrior's face softened and he smiled.

"Sokka," he said warmly.

He WAS glad to see me. I did make the right decision to come to him. "Hi, Dad!" I dashed across the tent and hugged him. And he hugged me back like neither one of us ever wanted to let go.

⊕ ⊕ ⊕

Over the next few days Dad helped me fit right in, just like I was one of the warriors who had left for battle with him all those years ago. I could see now that he was right to leave me behind at that time. I wasn't ready then, but I am now. Everything I have been through with Aang has made me the warrior I've become.

I got right to work helping Dad and his men set up a series of tangle mines along the bay to stop Fire Nation ships from getting to Ba Sing Se.

"The mines are filled with skunkfish and sea-weed," Dad explained. "When a ship detonates the mine, the seaweed tangles up the propellers and the foul fish smell forces the crew to abandon ship. I call it the stink 'n' sink."

"Good one, Dad!" Stink 'n' sink! I can defi-nitely see where I got my sense of humor!

Suddenly a warrior ran up to us. "Our scouts have spotted four Fire Nation ships."

"Bato, get these mines loaded up," Dad ordered. "The rest of you men, prepare for battle!"

What should I do? Should I go with the other men? I mean, even though I considered myself a warrior, I wasn't sure I was a warrior in Dad's eyes. Did he still see me as a little kid and expect me to stay behind? I didn't want to do the wrong thing. "Uh, what should I do, Dad?"

"Aren't you listening?" he said sternly. "I just said 'the rest of you men, prepare for battle!'"

He thinks I'm a man! I'm one of his warriors! I hurried to join the others, applied wolf battle paint to my face, strapped on my machete, and grabbed a war club.

"Ready to go knock some Fire Nation heads?" Dad asked.

"You don't know how much this means to me, Dad. I'll make you proud. And I'll finally prove to you what a great warrior I am."

Dad grasped my shoulder and squeezed gently. He looked right into my eyes and smiled. "Sokka, you don't have to prove anything to me. I'm already proud of you, and I've always known you're a great warrior."

"Really?"

"Why do you think I trusted you to look after our tribe when I left?"

Could this day get any better? I felt so proud—and so ready to fight the Fire Nation, right next to my father.

That's when Appa swooped down into our camp. And Aang's face said it all: the day had just turned bad. "This can't be good news," I said.

"Katara's in trouble," Aang said. "She needs our help."

I didn't need to hear any more. I hugged Dad tightly, then scrambled onto Appa's back and flew off. Looking down I could see the love in Dad's eyes as he watched me fly away. Then he turned and joined the other warriors on the Water Tribe ships setting out for battle. It felt good to know that he would have been proud to have me beside him on his ship.

⊕ ⊕ ⊕

"So what kind of trouble is Katara in?" I asked when the Water Tribe ships had faded from view.

"I don't know. In my vision I just knew she needed help."

Well, there was nothing to do but get back

to Ba Sing Se as fast as Appa could fly us.

Along the way we spotted Toph riding an Earthbending wave. We swooped down and picked her up.

"It was so great seeing my Dad again," I told her. "He treated me like a man, not a kid."

"I had a breakthrough myself," Toph told us. "I figured out how to bend metal."

"That's amazing, Toph! What about you, Aang?"

"I completely mastered the Avatar state."

It sounded like we'd all had pretty success—ful breaks—all except for Katara, apparently. I really hoped she was all right.

We landed in Ba Sing Se and hurried to the king's throne room.

"Katara's fine," the king told us. "She went off with the Kyoshi warriors."

Nothing to worry about—she's with Suki. But when we got back to our house we found Momo there by himself. He was agitated, jumping all over the place. She wasn't there. Maybe she really was in trouble.

Someone knocked at the door. When Toph

went to open it, I was shocked to see Zuko's uncle Iroh standing in the doorway!

"He's an old friend of mine," Toph said, before inviting him in.

I grabbed my war club. "I'm warning you. If you make one false move—"

"Princess Azula is in Ba Sing Se," Iroh said.

That's some really bad news.

"She must have Katara!" Aang said.

"She has captured my nephew as well."

"Then we'll have to work together to save Katara and Zuko," Aang announced.

Hold on—did I just hear Aang say we would work with Iroh to help save Zuko? That is SO wrong!

We then learned several things from a Dai Li agent Iroh had captured. "Azula is plotting to overthrow the Earth King," he told us. "And Katara and Zuko are in the crystal catacombs of Old Ba Sing Se, beneath the palace."

We hurried out to a courtyard near the palace, where Toph Earthbended a tunnel leading down.

We had two problems: We needed to

rescue Katara—and also that angry jerk Zuko—and we needed to warn the Earth King about Azula's coup. "I think we should split up," I said.

So Aang and Iroh headed down the tunnel while Toph and I went to warn the king. We spotted General How just in time to see a bunch of Dai Li agents surround and arrest him. "The coup has already started. We've got to get to the king right now!" I told Toph.

We burst into the throne room. There was the king surrounded by the Kyoshi warriors.

"Thank goodness we're in time!" I said. But something didn't feel right. I didn't recognize any of the girls. Where's Suki?

Then Ty Lee stepped forward and started flirting with me. While it was flattering and all, my heart was with Suki and—wait a second! What's going on?

"These aren't the real Kyoshi warriors!" Toph cried.

Ty Lee tried to block my chi but I managed to duck out of the way. That's when I saw that Azula was right next to the Earth King, ready to strike him with a Firebending move. We had no choice. We had to surrender or risk losing the king. The Dai Li hauled us away.

They locked Toph and me in an underground prison cell. The cell was made of metal, which they thought made it "Earthbender proof." But they had no idea that Toph had learned to bend metal. . . . Hey, if you're going to be locked in a metal prison cell, it's a good idea to have a Metalbender with you.

"See any Dai Li agents nearby?" Toph asked.

"Nope," I whispered. "All clear."

Toph bent open the metal bars of the cell and we stepped right through. After knocking down a few Dai Li guards, we hurried to the Earth King's cell. Toph did her Metalbending thing again and freed the king. "Come on, we've got to get you to safety!" I told him.

We rushed back through the tunnels and ran into Katara. In her arms she held Aang. His eyes were closed and he wasn't moving.

"Oh, no." What happened to Aang? He had to be all right. All of this meant nothing if Aang wasn't okay.

I had a million questions for Katara, but I

knew that getting out of Ba Sing Se was more important right then.

We returned to the surface and found Appa. Then Katara, Aang, Toph, the Earth King, and I took off. Once we were safely in the air, Katara used her Waterbending healing ability to help Aang. He opened his eyes and, although he was weak and groggy, it looked like he was going to be okay.

As we flew over the outer wall of Ba Sing Se, soaring away from the city, the Earth King looked down and said, "The Earth Kingdom has fallen."

Until that very moment it hadn't really hit me. The Earth King was leaving his city. Azula's coup attempt was successful. The Fire Nation now had control of Ba Sing Se, and with it, the entire Earth Kingdom.

We failed. I failed. What good is our information about the Fire Nation now? How in the world can we stop them? Will I ever see Dad again? Will anything ever go back to being normal? I wish I knew, but at the moment, I just don't have a clue.

LOOK FOR THESE BOOKS BASED ON NICKELODEON'S AVATAR: THE LAST AIRBENDER AT YOUR FAVORITE STORE!